SECOND BASE SECOND CHANCE

LINDA FAUSNET

Published by Wannabe Pride 2021

Editing by Linda Hill

Cover Design by Chuck DeKett

FIRST EDITION.

Library of Congress Control Number: 2021921943

❀ Created with Vellum

1

MATT

(The College Years)

I fell in love with Julia Frederick when we were sixteen years old.

Currently buzzing on alcohol and short of breath in the stifling Florida heat, I stared at her from across the crowded room of the rented house in South Beach. It was college spring break, and the party was in full swing. Try as I might, I could not tear my gaze away from the girl with the bright smile, long curly brown hair, and traffic-stopping hazel eyes. Still, I could sit here undressing Julia with my eyes only so long, considering her twin brother was sitting right next to me. Jerry had no clue about the naughty thoughts I had for his sister, and I'd best keep it that way.

Jerry, Julia, and I grew up together in rural Pennsylvania, and I could pinpoint the precise moment Julia went from my best friend's bratty sister to a desirable woman in my eyes. She was technically six minutes older than her brother, but Jerry and I still used to treat her like an annoying tagalong little sister. She'd always been rather fun to hang out with, though. A rough and tumble tomboy, she had fit in well with the rest of the guys in the neighborhood.

Then came the day in high school when Jerry and I sat in the stands, cheering her on as her softball team fought to win the championship. I didn't know what it was, but something struck me hard that day when Julia swung the bat and launched the ball down the right baseline. Perhaps it was partly due to our mutual love of sports. My own lifelong dream was to play professional baseball.

Dashing to first base, her long curly hair bouncing in her tight ponytail, she slid into first, safe by a fraction of a second. Fierce passion and triumph flashed in those hazel eyes, and just like that, I was hooked on her. Since that moment, no one else has ever compared to her in my eyes.

Julia was passionate about everything she did. She was the living embodiment of the old adage of work hard, play hard. I'd always had the work hard part down, the play part was a struggle for me.

Jerry turned his head, and I followed his gaze. It seemed he had his eye on a hottie as well.

"Go talk to him," I said, tipping my beer bottle in the hot guy's direction. I was the first person Jerry came out to when he was eighteen years old. Though I was ashamed of it now, I'd been pretty freaked out at the time. I managed to stumble through some halfway comforting words about how everything was going to be okay and his father wouldn't be *that* upset, which we'd both known was a lie. Inwardly, I had the stereotypical guy reaction, getting all squeamish and uncomfortable and worrying if it meant he was attracted to me. God, I'd been an idiot. Fortunately, it hadn't taken me long to come to my senses and realize Jerry was the same person I'd always known, only he was attracted to men instead of women. Now, a few years later, I would often scan the room for hot guys for him the same way he scoped out the ladies for me.

"Well, would you look at that," I said, chuckling. "You've established eye contact."

"Sure have," Jerry said with a grin as he locked eyes with a blue-eyed surfer-type guy. "Catch you later."

He got up and walked toward Surfer Dude, whose smile widened when he saw my buddy approach. With his longish, curly brown hair and the same hazel eyes as Julia, my pal was a catch for sure.

Jerry's absence gave me the opportunity to go back to staring at his sister, who was the life of the party as usual. Despite the crowd and the noise, I could still hear her throaty laugh rise up over the din. Beer in hand, she joked around with her friends.

Needing another drink, I reluctantly got up from my comfortable seat to toss my empty bottle into a recycle bin and grab another beer from the cooler. Lucky for me, my chair was still vacant when I got back. The place was packed with people, but as always, I was the only one not talking to anybody. I was glad the spring break trip was almost over. Pathetic as it was, I was more comfortable being at school than at a party.

At school I had my classes and, most importantly, baseball. I'd been awarded a baseball scholarship to the University of Central Pennsylvania, and I hoped like hell I'd get drafted to the minors after next year, when I graduated. Between being laser focused on baseball and keeping my A-average with a major in computer science, I didn't have much time for a social life. Jerry attended a college in Delaware, which was a four-hour drive away, so it wasn't like I had him to hang out with very often. Though I knew plenty of people at the university, they were mostly acquaintances as opposed to actual friends.

Sighing out loud, I forced myself to quit staring longingly at Julia. She wasn't looking in my direction, but for all I knew other people had noticed me eying her up like some creep. My head spun a bit, and I realized I'd already drained the beer I'd just opened. I needed some air, so I got up and stepped onto the balcony. There were already three people out there, but they were just putting out their cigarettes to go back inside.

I grimaced at my first deep breath after stepping outside —stale cigarette smoke instead of the fresh ocean breeze. Once the smoke dissipated, I drew in another deep breath of the night air. This time, I could smell the sea. It helped clear my beer-buzzed brain a little. I figured I'd take a few minutes to sober up and then stumble back to my hotel room. Jerry was probably about to get lucky, so there was no reason for me to stay at this party any longer.

The sliding door opened up behind me, and I took that as my cue to get going. I was in no mood to contend with some horny couple who only wanted to make out or a bunch of frat boys who would probably light up some joints. I turned around and my heart seized in my chest.

Julia.

I hoped to God my poker face was halfway believable. She'd always been perceptive, and it was a wonder she hadn't already figured out how I felt about her. Julia had always treated me as a friend, not to mention her brother's *best* friend. She'd never given any indication of wanting anything more. I saw no reason to clue her in that I was hopelessly in love with her, which would undoubtedly ruin our friendship. She would never see me as anything more than a loyal yet really boring and highly studious pal. A firecracker like her needed a much more exciting man in her life.

"What are you doing out here all by yourself?" she asked, taking a spot close enough for our arms to touch at the balcony railing.

"Jerry found some hot surfer guy to hook up with," I said bluntly, and Julia threw her head back and laughed.

"Good for him," she said with the smile that lit the way wherever she went. Julia had no problem discussing her brother's sex life. Jerry, however, couldn't stand the thought of his sister being sexually active and would literally stick his fingers in his ears when anyone mentioned it. Which, of course, encouraged us all to joke about it constantly, with Julia being the biggest offender. Nobody enjoyed torturing Jerry more than she did.

Jerry wasn't the only one being tortured. It felt like a knife in my chest whenever I was forced to hear about Julia's healthy, active sex life. She'd had a few steady boyfriends, but I knew she wasn't currently seeing anyone. Still, she was just as likely as her brother to pick up a stranger at a party and have wild and hopefully safe sex. As with my reaction to Jerry being gay, I'd picked up some outdated views from my family when it came to women. My dad taught me that any woman who slept around was a slut. Now, I shuddered just hearing that word, especially when it came to the woman I loved. Being close with Julia had shown me the evils of the double standard. She was doing exactly what the guys were doing, only they got praised for it. I admired her strength and the way she did what she wanted and didn't care what other people thought. Despite my admiration for her female empowerment, it still felt like a gut punch when I had to hear about her being with another guy.

"There's plenty of action in there for a good-looking stud

like you, ya know," Julia said, turning around to look through the glass doors at the partygoers. "No reason you have to go back to your hotel room alone, which you were just about to do if I know you."

Chuckling, I said, "Guilty. Figured I might as well get some rest since we gotta head back tomorrow."

Julia shook her head. "The way I see it, you might as well live it up tonight since we have to go back tomorrow."

"So go live it up instead of hanging out with a wet blanket like me."

"You are not a wet blanket," she said, gently rubbing my arm and slowly driving me crazy. "But it probably would do you good to cut loose for once. Come on, look."

Julia grabbed me by the shoulder and turned me around to face the party. "There are tons of pretty girls in there right now looking for one last fling before they go back to school. One more wild time. This is your lucky night, Matt. You could have your pick of the ladies."

I shook my head, wishing I had another beer to down right about now. "I don't think so. Not exactly my scene."

"I've known you my whole life, and I still don't know exactly what your scene is. I don't think *you* know. At least, you don't know what to do with yourself outside of the baseball field or the library."

Shrugging, I said, "You're not wrong."

"I swear, in the two years I've been in college with you, I don't think I've even seen you with a girl."

Julia shook her head, and I sighed. While I was working toward a four-year bachelor's degree, she was working on a shorter associate's degree and would graduate this year. God, I would miss her.

"Seriously," she said, her voice growing quieter. "I really haven't seen you with any girls."

Terror seized in my chest as Julia inched dangerously close to my most private secret. Something nobody knew about me.

"Matt," she said, tugging on my arm. "You're not gay, are you?"

I let out a breath. She hadn't guessed my secret. Also, if she was questioning my sexuality, she clearly had no idea how I felt about her. Good.

"No, I'm not gay."

"I mean, you would tell me, right?" she asked, eyes opened wide.

"Of course I would. You of all people would have no problem with that."

Julia had known Jerry was gay before he had, I was pretty sure, and she was a big believer in "living your truth" as she called it. She always said as long as you weren't hurting anybody, you should be who you are, and screw everybody else if they didn't like it.

"Right," she said, looking confused; hurt, even. Clearly, she knew there was something I wasn't telling her. She fell silent for a few seconds, then asked quietly, "Matt, are you a virgin?"

I felt my face flush a deep, burning red. So much for my poker face. There was no sense even attempting to lie to Julia.

"Oh. I'm sorry," she said somberly. "I didn't know."

Then she burst out laughing, rendering my humiliation total and complete.

Pulling me into a tight hug, she said, "No, no. I'm not laughing at you, Matt. I swear. I just ..." She started giggling again. "I heard my own words as I said them out loud." In a mock serious tone, she repeated them. "Oh, I'm sorry. I didn't know."

I refused to look at her and for a moment, I seriously considered jumping over the balcony.

"I didn't mean to act like somebody died or something. That was dumb of me, and I'm sorry. This really isn't a big deal." Wrapping her arm around me, she rested her head on my shoulder. "I love you so much, Matt."

It wasn't the first time she'd said that. In fact, Julia said it all the time. That was just her way—to always be open with her feelings. The total opposite of me.

Lifting her head, she said, "Well, I know it's not for religious reasons. Are you just not interested? Maybe you're asexual."

"I am *not* asexual."

"Some people are, Matt. Nothing wrong with that," she said firmly. I couldn't help grinning as she encouraged me to "live my truth" as an asexual person, should that be the case. Julia was the kind of friend everyone should have. Not only did she accept everyone for who they were, she celebrated people for their differences.

"Fine. But I am not one of those people."

"So you *do* want to have sex."

My muscles tensed. This whole thing was so embarrassing, and she was the last person on the planet I wanted to discuss this with. Jerry was my best friend, and even he didn't know. I'd been out on a few dates, and he'd just assumed I'd scored. He was always winking and nudging me afterward. Unlike straight guys, he had little interest in the details of my sexual encounters, so we never discussed it much further.

Gripping the guardrail of the balcony, I said grimly, "Can we please just change the subject?"

Julia gently rubbed my back. "It really isn't a big deal."

"Yes, it is. It's pathetic. I'm a junior in college. Can you imagine if the guys on the team knew? All they talk about is getting puss— I—I mean, getting laid."

She laughed and kept massaging my back. I always watched my language around her, even though she rarely got offended by anything.

"There's no way those guys could possibly know. You are so *sexy,* Matt. And you don't even know it. You don't see the girls who check you out all the time. But I see them." Her voice was filled with deep pride. "Just to be clear, you don't want to be a virgin anymore, right? Because you know I'm on your side no matter what's right for you. Just because lots of people at college sleep around doesn't mean you have to do it too. It's different for everybody. Some people wait until marriage. Some people never do it. And that's totally okay, and it's nobody else's business."

"Well, I hate being a virgin. It's not like it was something I planned."

Julia nodded thoughtfully. "You just work so much all the time. Baseball and school and all that."

"Pretty much." I sighed bitterly. "And now I feel like I'm so old that when I do take a woman to bed, I'll make a fool of myself because I won't know what I'm doing. It's fine to be awkward and terrible at sex when you're sixteen years old, but I'm almost twenty-one."

Laughing, she said, "Oh yeah. You're such an old man." Then, as breezily as if discussing what to have for lunch, she said, "You should do it with me."

It took me several seconds to fully register her words.

"What?" I asked incredulously.

"You should have sex with me. I can be your first."

Shaking my head in disbelief, I said, "That's crazy."

"No, it's really not when you think about it. I'm not

dating anybody right now, and it's my last night of vacation. I wanted one last fling anyway."

Julia was trying to do me a favor while making it sound like I would be doing her one. She was crafty that way. She could trick you into letting her help you. If we did sleep together, the pleasure would most assuredly be all mine. No way did I have anything to offer her.

"That's sweet of you, but it's too crazy. You're one of my best friends."

"Exactly," she said, brushing her luscious brown curls off her face. "You're safe with me. Nobody will ever have to know about it. You're gonna do fine, but you can get any awkwardness out of the way so you'll be ready when you meet the right woman for you."

You are the right woman for me. I'm just not the right man for you.

Julia's back rub had relaxed me a little, but now my body was more tense than ever. The idea of getting through my bumbling first sexual experience with the woman I loved was one hell of a lot of pressure.

It also felt like a once-in-a-lifetime opportunity that was awfully hard to pass up.

Drawing in a deep breath, I tried to think clearly. I needed to use my brain and not my heart, nor other body parts, to make this decision. Julia wasn't drunk, nor was she naive and inexperienced. She was a grown woman, and she knew exactly what she was getting into.

"Stop overthinking it and do something spontaneous for once in your life," Julia said, smiling at my furrowed brow and stern expression. I was wound pretty tight and we both knew it. "It's our vacation. What happens in South Beach stays in South Beach. We'll go back to your hotel room where we can have some privacy and take our time. Nobody will ever know, and the pressure will finally be off you."

I turned to face the ocean. Watching the waves roll in, I tried to contemplate all the pros and cons. But I didn't get very far.

"Come on. Let's go," Julia said, grabbing my arm and pulling me back into the crowded party room.

2

MATT

I could not believe I'd let Julia talk me into this. Not that it had taken much cajoling for me to agree to sex with the woman of my dreams, but still, part of me worried that this was insane and that one or both of us would regret it later. But even in my serious, practical mind, there seemed to be more reasons to do this than not.

Though I wished I could be as evolved and free-thinking as Julia Frederick when it came to things like societal pressure, I simply wasn't. The fact was my virginity caused me deep shame. I was thoroughly sick of feeling that way, and I wanted to shed my virginity as soon as humanly possible. I was scared to death of humiliating myself in front of my sweet Julia, but I also loved her too much to pass up a chance to be with her.

Jerry was still chatting up Surfer Dude as we headed out, so I told him his sister was a little too tipsy and I was gonna take her back to the hotel. I just didn't say *which* hotel. Guilt surged through me when Jerry thanked me for taking care of her.

He trusted me. The poor guy had absolutely no idea I

was heading back to my hotel room to defile his sister. I felt awful, but as with most guys who were about to get laid, I didn't let anything stop me.

Fortunately, my hotel was just a short walk away, so we didn't have to talk much. I opened the door to the room, ushered Julia in, and made sure the door was firmly locked once we were inside. After that, I was at a total loss on how to proceed. Julia took the lead, which was embarrassing but also comforting at the same time.

She sat down on the bed and smiled at me. "I can't help feeling we need to do this quick before you change your mind."

"Don't worry," I said, my face tight with stress. "I don't think quick will be the problem."

"Come here," she said softly, patting the spot next to her on the bed. I sat down stiffly. "I know it's useless to tell you not to be nervous, but please try to relax. This might even be *fun*, ya know."

Turning to face her, I took a moment to gaze at those hazel eyes I adored. Out of habit, I avoided looking down and staring at her breasts, but I knew what they looked like. At least, I knew what the top of her cleavage looked like when she wore low-cut shirts. My cock stiffened just thinking about it. Julia was, without question, the most attractive woman I'd ever known, and only part of it was her physical beauty. I was completely and utterly attracted to *her*. All of her.

She took hold of my hand and placed it on one of her breasts. My body tensed. As much as I longed to touch her, it all felt new and strange. I'd touched women before. Fooled around with a few in the car when I was in high school. But this was *Julia Frederick*. Until now, I'd only dreamed of touching her.

Gently, she put her arm around my neck and pulled me in for a kiss. After a brief second to recover from my surprise, I kissed her back. Even as it was happening, I could hardly believe it was real. Somehow, I'd wound up in a hotel room making out with the woman I'd loved from afar since we were teenagers. Julia moaned softly in her throat, which bolstered my confidence a bit. We kissed for a moment or two before she broke it off.

"I know this might feel a little strange because we're such good friends," Julia said.

"Yeah," I said, grimacing slightly at my least favorite F-word when it came from her lips. She was right, though. We'd been children together for God's sake. I flashed back on all those late nights playing outside in our neighborhood. It didn't exactly help the mood.

"We'll always be friends," she said, tracing my chin with her finger. "But tonight, I want you to think of me as your lover."

"Okay," I managed to croak. The sultry sound of her voice and that look of desire in her eyes reminded me that Julia was indeed a woman now. My lover. If only for tonight.

She kissed me again, then she pulled my shirt off over my head.

"*Damn,* you look good," she said, eying my chest. "You are an athlete, that's for sure."

Julia's approval of my body eased my nerves slightly. She might have said that just to encourage me, but I did work out a lot, and I was pretty muscular. Maybe she was legitimately turned on by me. God, I hoped so.

After a brief moment of silence, she said, "Just touch me in whatever way feels natural to you."

"Oh. Right." I couldn't expect her to do everything.

I pulled off her shirt to reveal her black bra underneath.

I sucked in a breath, still adjusting to the fact that I was allowed to look.

She's your lover right now, not just your friend.

Still, it was an effort to allow myself to feel her chest. But I did it.

Julia closed her eyes and moaned encouragingly. "I love that."

She opened her eyes, arched her back, then reached around to unclasp her bra.

"I do that for lots of guys, not just 'cause you're inexperienced. Bras are hard to get off," she said with a laugh. Though she meant to be helpful, that just reminded me of all the other guys she'd been with. Who were no doubt way better in bed than I was going to be tonight.

Shaking off the thought, I pulled her bra the rest of the way off. She scooted closer to me, and I massaged her breasts with my hands. Feeling her body was incredibly erotic, making it hard to go slowly.

Moaning again, she said, "Feels so good when you do that." Then she murmured in my ear, "You're getting me so wet."

My spirits soared. Julia was always kind and encouraging, but she never lied. If she said I was getting her aroused, then I was. Words of praise from the woman I loved emboldened me.

I took her by the hand and stood her up and we finished undressing each other. At last, we were both naked. Pulling her close, I kissed her deeply, pressing my erection against her. She moaned louder.

I kissed down her neck toward her breasts, and then took one in my mouth and sucked.

"Oh God, that's good," she said in a husky voice. She guided my right hand toward her entrance and helped me put two fingers inside her. She was drenched. "Do you feel how ready I am for you?"

"Yes," I panted. Our sensual foreplay excited me so much, I was a little afraid I would come just from that. Drawing in a deep breath, I fought to quash my sudden terror at that thought.

"Lemme go grab a condom," she said in my ear.

Jesus. Thank God she knew what the hell she was doing because I had completely forgotten about protection.

She handed me the shiny square packet from her purse and said, "Take your time putting it on. Shouldn't be too hard, so to speak. And if you want to look really sexy, tear the packet open with your teeth."

"With my luck, I'd rip the condom," I said, and she laughed softly.

I was acutely aware of her watching me as I stretched the condom over my dick.

"You're pretty big," she said huskily. "I always thought you would be."

So she's thought about my cock before?

Worrying about getting the condom on right deflated me slightly, but one look at Julia's perfect, naked body literally straightened out the problem right away.

"Are you ready?" she asked gently.

I drew in a breath, feeling well past ready yet scared to go on at the same time.

"Don't overthink it. Just do it. Do *me*, Matt. 'Cuz you got me so turned on, I can't wait much longer," she said, hazel eyes flashing. She lay down on the bed for me.

Oh God, is this really happening?

Julia Frederick was lying spread-eagled on a bed waiting for me to take her. And take her I would.

I climbed on top of her and started kissing her, and she

eagerly kissed me back. Suddenly struck with indecision and lack of confidence, I found myself hesitating to go all the way. I wasn't exactly sure how to go about it, was terrified of screwing it all up.

"Just slip yourself inside me when you're ready," Julia said, sounding breathless. She sure as hell sounded ready, and that was all the invitation I needed.

I positioned myself at her entrance and slid myself inside of her. The burst of pleasure was more intense than anything I had ever experienced before. My own fist had nothing on a woman's vagina. I couldn't stifle my groan of sheer bliss as I began to move in and out of Julia.

"Oh God, that's good," she said, her eyes rolling back in her head before she closed them.

I closed mine, too, realizing I would need to concentrate on not coming too fast. I thrust harder. She moaned louder.

"You're doing great, Matt."

"You don't have to say that," I said through clenched teeth.

Don't come yet. Not yet. Not yet.

"I mean it. That's good ... that's ... really ... good."

Her ankles dug into my ass, driving me half out of my mind. I knew this once-in-a-lifetime event would be over all too quickly, and I wanted to savor every single second.

I'm having sex. I'm actually doing it. And with Julia Frederick.

I grunted hard with effort.

"Don't hold back, Matt. Just let go. Come. I want to feel you *come* inside me."

At her command, I came and came hard, groaning loudly.

My orgasm went on and on. When it was over, I gazed into the lovely eyes of the most beautiful soul I had ever known. I was so physically spent and emotionally vulnerable that I damn near blurted out that I was in love with her. Thank God almighty she spoke first.

"You did it," Julia said with a warm and loving smile, her voice filled with pride.

"Yeah. Yeah, I guess I did," I said, reluctantly pulling out of her. I slid the condom off, grabbed a tissue from the box on the nightstand to wrap it in, and tossed it in the trash. Then I lay back down beside Julia.

She rolled onto her side and gazed at me. "Matt, that was amazing. I never would have known that was your first time if you hadn't told me."

I scoffed audibly.

"I mean it," she insisted.

"It was so fast."

"That's not unusual. Really. Only in the movies and in porno does it take a long time. In real life, sometimes it's fast. Sometimes it's slow."

I was suddenly filled with deep gratitude that Julia had been my first. It had gone so much smoother than I'd expected. She built me up the whole time and never made me feel stupid or inadequate for my inexperience. It was a beautiful reminder of why I loved her so much.

"Thank you for this, Julia. It's such a relief, in every possible way, that we did this."

"I'm so glad," she said with a smile. "You were wonderful."

"No, I wasn't. You didn't come. Doubt you even came close."

Julia shrugged. "I never have an orgasm during regular missionary sex."

"Oh. Should we have tried a different position?" I asked, feeling terrible that I might have disappointed her.

"Well," she said, sitting up in the bed. "Maybe, but it's not just that. I'm like most women. The only way I can have an orgasm is if you rub my clit." Her unabashed way of speaking would have made her a good sex ed teacher. "Sometimes if I'm on top, I can grind on a guy and that does the trick. Otherwise, I need more direct stimulation."

"That makes sense."

"Yeah," she said. "Again, only in movies does a woman have a screaming orgasm while the guy is thrusting in and out of her. Real life is different."

I nodded, mulling over this information like there was going to be a test later. Crazy how nobody really tells you how to please a woman. Losing my virginity to Julia had been a great idea after all. Who else would have patiently explained such things to me without making me feel like an idiot? She had that way about her. She was brazen and outspoken, and yet she put everyone at ease at the same time.

"Well then," I said, realizing that the first test of my new knowledge was right now. I had a beautiful, naked, and aroused woman who needed sexual release. "I need to stimulate you directly."

I winced inwardly at the decidedly unsexy words I'd used. Clearly, I hadn't gotten the hang of dirty talk yet.

Smiling at me, she said, "You don't have to do that."

"Yes. I do."

Julia lay down on her back and gazed at me, her sweet, pink nipples erect. I'd felt with my fingers how wet she'd been. There was no way in hell I would leave her unsatisfied.

Running my hand over her naked breasts, I gently tweaked her nipples, making her moan.

"You can't tell me you don't want it. That you don't *need*

it," I said, impressed with how husky my voice sounded. I was getting better at seduction already.

"You're right," Julia said in a breathy voice. "I do need it."

She lowered her gaze to my chest, and I watched her eyes flash slightly as she stared at my muscles. My confidence soared again. She made me feel like a *man* when she looked at me like that. I wished I could make love to her again. Better, longer this time. But I knew it was not to be. The first time had been so pleasurable that I knew it would take a while to physically gear up again. Though I felt bad about that, I had a feeling if I'd voiced those concerns out loud, Julia would have said only in the movies and porno could a guy get rock hard again two minutes after having sex.

I pressed my lips to hers, both for foreplay and because I simply wanted to kiss her again. She kissed me back hungrily, and I knew she must be desperate for release by now. I felt more confident about pleasuring her with my hand. I had fingered girls before, though it had been a while.

Slipping two fingers inside her, I began thrusting in and out of her, making her cry out.

"Oh God, that's good," she said, closing her eyes.

I loved watching her face as I pleasured her. For once, she didn't have to provide sexual instruction for me, and she could just enjoy her turn. I gently thumbed her clit, which made her cry out louder.

"Oh God, yes. Yes ... yes ..."

I sped up the rhythm of my finger motion based on her cries.

Then she grew quiet, her mouth opened in a silent O. I could tell she was close.

"Matt! *Oh!*" Julia cried at last, her body spasming with her climax.

I knew I would never forget the sound of her screaming my name when she came. I'd fantasized about it countless times, and I could hardly believe it had actually happened.

"Mmmmm," she said lazily. Julia reached for me, pulling me close to her body.

We lay there together, naked bodies pressed against each other, and it was the happiest moment of my entire life. That was when I knew, really *knew*, I wanted to spend the rest of my life with her.

Was it possible she could ever feel that way about me?

I needed to just ask her. Being so close to her all the time at school and casually hanging out with her and Jerry on the weekends was crushing the life out of my heart. Either way, I simply had to know if she could ever think of me as more than a friend.

But I couldn't ask her right this moment. She might think I was just feeling vulnerable because I'd just lost my virginity to her. No. Asking her out on a proper date was a fully clothed type of question.

Julia looked up at me with her sex-tousled hair and luscious eyes filled with hazy sexual satisfaction. "That was amazing, Matt. All of it. You should be proud of yourself."

"Thanks," I said, my face heating. Gazing at her, I couldn't find the words to tell her how grateful I was for her kindness, and not just for tonight. I was grateful to Julia just for being *Julia*.

I was still searching for the words when, unfortunately, she got up to get dressed.

"Needless to say," she said as she slipped her shirt over her head, not bothering with her bra, "Jerry can never know about this."

"Right," I said, guilt squeezing in my gut at the memory of Jerry's trusting face when I told him I was going to take care of his sister.

Which, technically, I guess I had.

"There's no need to tell anybody about this, Matt," she said softly with a smile. "I mean, it wouldn't do me any harm for people to know I had sex with one of the hottest baseball players on the University of Central Pennsylvania team."

Her compliment thrilled me. I loved that she'd called me a hot baseball player. For me, there was no higher compliment.

"But you know Jerry would lose his mind, and I know how bad you felt about being a virgin," Julia said gently. "So going forward, I'll just be some random girl you banged on spring break that you can tell all your friends about."

"Julia!" I said, horrified.

She laughed, a rich, throaty sound. "I know you don't really think of me that way."

You have no idea.

"The point is, this is your story to tell however you want to. You know I'll be cool with whatever you say."

"Yeah. I know."

I got up and quickly got dressed. Once she was ready to go, she wrapped me in a warm hug. I could feel her braless breasts pressing against me and what do you know? I was getting hard again already.

"You were wonderful tonight. You're gonna make any woman who's lucky enough to have you very happy, and you're gonna leave her *incredibly* satisfied."

Julia graced me with that sexy, hazy look again. She always knew just what to say to make me feel good about myself.

I want you to be that allegedly lucky woman, Julia.

With one last peck on the lips from her, she was gone.

Back on campus on Monday, I had to somehow gather the courage to ask her if she wanted to be more than friends with only this one-time benefit.

And then, whatever her answer, I would have to deal with the consequences.

THOUGH I WAS sure it was largely psychological, I felt like more of a man when I returned to school after spring break. I had more of a spring in my step, and somehow, I felt more like I belonged here, both on campus and on the baseball team. My new confidence seemed to have a positive effect on my athletic performance. During my first practice after losing my virginity, I asked our ace pitcher to toss his best stuff my way to see what I could do with it. I'd always struggled with the changeup pitch, but not this time. I saw the ball better than ever and launched a few of his toughest pitches right out of the damned park.

If having sex with Julia helped this much, I couldn't imagine what having her as my girlfriend might do for my life.

Rather than being tired, I felt energized after baseball practice, so I went for a long run. That was one of my favorite ways to work off nervous energy. Running invigorated me and got my blood pumping, and it gave me time to think. The university campus was gorgeous, and my regular runs here were incredibly scenic with huge, green mountains as the backdrop. I ran hard, my heart pounding and sweat pouring. It felt like I was running toward my future, which hopefully involved a career in Major League Baseball and Julia by my side.

3

JULIA

After I finished my last class of the morning, I headed over to Café Shirley on the south campus to grab some lunch. Though I usually enjoyed my Introductory Soil Science class, I was still dragging from spring break. This was the first day back after a rather wild week in South Beach, and I was still adjusting to reality.

I paid for my meal and scanned the lunchroom for an open seat. That's when I saw Matt sitting all alone at a table next to the window. At six feet two inches, he looked huge hunching over the table, nose buried in some computer science book. Grinning, I clutched my food tray and hurried over to him.

My stomach tingled when Matt lifted his head. With his deep blue eyes, dirty-blond hair, and chiseled athletic physique, my childhood friend had grown up to be quite a looker. I wasn't sure exactly when Matt had gone from dorky neighborhood kid to sexy man in my eyes. Had he not told me, I would never have guessed in a million years that he was still a virgin. Well, at least he was until last week when I took his innocence.

"Oh, h—hey Julia," he said when he saw me, his face turning red. Matt could be so adorable sometimes.

I set my tray on the table and plopped down on the seat across from him.

"You don't have to be uncomfortable around me just because we saw each other naked and had terrific sex a few days ago," I said with a smile.

Avoiding my gaze, he closed his computer book and shuffled his tray to make room for me.

"Matt," I said, reaching over and taking his hand in mine. I lowered my voice and said, "It was such an honor to be your first. I mean that. And I don't want you to be uncomfortable around me. Ever. You're one of my best friends."

Matt nodded, and he seemed to relax a bit.

"You gonna miss me next year?" I asked. I would get my Associate's Degree in Turf Management at the end of this semester. I loved working with plants and grass and everything outdoors, and I had big dreams of doing groundskeeping work in professional sports.

"Of course I'm going to miss you," he said, those serious blue eyes filled with genuine sadness.

I worried how Matt would do without me on campus next year. Sometimes I thought if it weren't for me, he wouldn't talk to anybody. It wasn't that he was shy, exactly. More like he was so utterly focused on baseball and schoolwork that he tended to ignore everything else. No wonder he'd never been with a woman before. With his good looks and quiet charm, he could snap his fingers and the panties would drop. But he had to talk to women first.

"I'm happy for you," he said. "But I do wish you weren't going so far away."

"Yeah. I get that," I said and then took a bite of my meatball sub. Though I would miss my friends and family here in Pennsylvania, I was incredibly psyched about my internship with the Triple-A Kentucky Mad Batters minor league team. Since I was just starting out, I would have taken a groundskeeping internship anywhere, but I was thrilled to have landed a baseball job instead of some stupid golf course. "It would have been cool to get a job closer. Still, there's something exciting about going somewhere totally new where I don't know anybody."

Matt chuckled. "You would say that. For lots of people, moving to a different state where you don't know anybody would be a nightmare. But you make friends everywhere you go. Always have."

He grinned at me. I knew he was proud of me for landing that internship, and that meant a lot to me. Though he was my brother's best friend, Matt and I had gotten closer while we were in college. I knew we would always be in each other's lives, no matter where our careers took us.

"I really do appreciate everything you did for me," he said, making eye contact this time rather than shyly looking away. It was kinda hot.

"Believe me, it was no sacrifice having amazing sex with an incredibly handsome man."

Matt gazed intently into my eyes, and I felt my heart skip a beat. The man was devastatingly gorgeous, and he could be so intense sometimes. Though his intensity could be sexy, I wished for his sake he would lighten up once in a while.

"I really hope you get drafted next year," I told him.

"Me too. If I don't, at least I'll still have my degree in computer science."

"Yes, you will. And I hope you never have to use it."

He grinned. "Me too, Julia."

Matt worked hard to get good grades, taking his fallback

career of computer science seriously. He took everything seriously, but baseball was the most important thing in his life. He was a man of few words, but I could see the passion sparkle in his eyes when he was on the ballfield. He wanted to be a pro ballplayer so damned much, and nobody deserved it more than he did. I hoped with all my heart that he would make it to the majors someday.

"After I graduate, are you gonna sit by yourself at lunch every day or are you gonna get up the nerve to ask a pretty girl to sit with you?"

Matt shrugged, and I was afraid I already knew the answer.

"You deserve to find somebody amazing to be with. Don't be afraid to strike up a conversation with a girl. In no time, you'll find a woman to try out your new bedroom skills with."

"Skills," he scoffed.

"You were great, Matt," I said, vividly recalling the delicious sensation of his huge cock sliding into me. "I really mean it. You've got a big dick, and I was amazed at the way you found a pleasurable rhythm almost right away."

Matt scrutinized my face, clearly wanting to believe me.

"Seriously. If you were that good your first time ... Any woman would be really lucky to be your lover. That, and I really want you to meet somebody special *now*. Before you make it big as a hotshot MLB player and you have women chasing after you because you're so handsome and you have lots of money. I want you to be with a woman who loves you for you."

"Oh, yeah. I'm sure the girls on campus will be lining up for a computer science nerd."

"Nothing wrong with being a computer science nerd,

but that's not you anyway. That's just Plan B. You're a baseball player. That's who you really are."

That familiar spark lit up his gorgeous blue eyes.

"That's true," he said with a smile.

"I want you to promise me that you will look up from your schoolbooks once in a while and at least attempt to find Ms. Right," I said firmly.

Matt swallowed hard. "Yeah. Well ... about that ..."

"You have somebody in mind already, don't you?"

He nodded, nervousness in his eyes.

"Oh, that's wonderful! I wouldn't even mind if you were fantasizing about her when you were with me," I said with a smile.

"No guy in his right mind would think of somebody else while he was with you, Julia," he said sternly.

"Thanks. I appreciate you saying that. Matt, whoever this girl is you've got your eye on, you gotta go for it!" I slapped the table to emphasize my words, startling him a bit.

"You really think so?"

"Yes. Absolutely. Without question."

Matt fell silent, and I knew he was overthinking again.

"Some things you can't just think out, Matthew Jovey. You have to feel them. If there's some woman out there who's caught your eye, talk to her. Just strike up a conversation. Ask her out. It's not as hard as you're making it out to be. Worst-case scenario, she'll say no. But Matt." I grabbed his hand and kissed it. "I'm telling you. You are a *catch*. As long as this girl isn't seeing somebody else, there's no way she'll say no."

Matt nodded uncertainly. He was already a nervous wreck just thinking about asking this girl out. I could see the panic in his eyes. If he could only see what the rest of the world saw when they looked at him—a hunky athlete with brooding, deep blue eyes who exuded sex appeal without even knowing it, which of course made him all the more attractive.

"I—I guess I could try." His statement sounded more like a question. I could just imagine my sweet, hulking friend tentatively asking a woman out on a date. For real, you could swoon with a guy like that. Anybody would.

"Of course you can."

"Julia, I—I ..." he began as he fiddled with his napkin.

"What? Ask me anything. I want to help in any way I can."

Matt raked a hand through his hair. Seriously, he could *not* be more adorable.

"There is something I wanted to ask you. It might sound kinda crazy."

"You can ask me anything. You know that."

"Yeah. I do know that," he said quietly.

"Okay. So ask."

"Never mind," he said with a dismissive wave of his hand.

"Matthew!"

"Just forget it. Really."

"You are so maddening sometimes."

"I know," he said apologetically.

Sighing deeply, I said, "As much as I would love to sit here and browbeat you until you open up, I gotta get to class."

Eyes downcast, Matt looked like he was disappointed in himself.

"I love you, you know," I said.

He nodded. He never said "I love you" back. He just wasn't the lovey-dovey type. But I didn't mind. He loved me in his own way, and that was cool with me. Matt was as loyal a friend as they came. He didn't have to say the words. He showed how he felt with his actions and the way he always had my back.

"Believe me. You're gonna make some woman very happy someday."

Matt smiled weakly. He clearly didn't believe me, but I knew I was right.

AFTER MY TURFGRASS Insect Pest Management class, I wandered over to the baseball field. It was such a nice day that I couldn't bear to spend another second indoors. The college baseball team, the Falcons, were milling around and getting ready for practice. Matt was there, of course. He was always one of the first to arrive at practice. Already working on his swing, he was laser focused and hadn't seen me yet.

I bent down and touched the dirt, breathing in the smell of the freshly cut turf. My stomach quivered with excitement knowing that soon I would be permanently out of the classroom and onto the playing field. I could hardly wait to get up early in the morning and head to the ballpark to help prep the field for game day.

"I like a girl who's not afraid to get her hands dirty," came a deep male voice from just above me.

Shielding my eyes from the sun, I recognized the guy with dark wavy hair, brown eyes, and those dimples that were famous all over campus. Kyle Nolan. Star pitcher of the Falcons.

I stood up and put my hands on my hips. "Oh honey. I'm not afraid to get anything dirty."

He grinned and extended his hand. "Kyle Nolan."

I wiped my dirty hands on my pants before shaking his

hand. "I know who you are. Starter with a 2.5 ERA. Known for your cutter and slider pitches. You really know how to make a baseball move and screw with the batter's head."

"Very good," he said, his sexy grin widening. "Nice grip."

I smiled. My mom had taught me to always have a firm handshake, and it had served me well. Made people take me more seriously, which was crucial in my line of work.

"Julia Frederick."

"So what do you do when you're not playing in the dirt?" Kyle asked.

"I'll have you know that I play in the dirt professionally. Or at least I will when I graduate this year. Getting my degree in Turf Management. Then I'm gonna be a groundskeeper intern with the Kentucky Mad Batters."

"No kidding," Kyle said, his brown eyes wide. "What are they, Single-A?"

I shook my head. "Nope. Triple-A."

"Damn. One step down from the majors. Not bad for your first job outta college."

"Right? I can't believe it. I'm so excited."

"So is that what you want to do? Sports groundskeeping?"

"Yup."

"That is very cool," he said, sounding impressed. "Nothing sexier than a girl who knows sports."

I grimaced at that. "We're not a rare breed, you know. Lots of women are into sports. They're even known to *play* them from time to time."

He winced. "Right. Sorry. I didn't mean for that to sound sexist. I just meant it's cool to meet a girl with the same interests as me."

I laughed to show there were no hard feelings. We stood there talking shop for a while. I told him about my adventures in softball and how we made it to the championship last year. He told me all about his dreams of pitching in the big leagues. It really was fun talking with somebody who shared the same interests.

"Can you imagine?" Kyle said, his eyes dreamy like Matt's when he spoke of baseball. "I know it's silly, but I fantasize about tossing a no-hitter or better yet, a perfect game. The crowd chanting my name. Baseball immortality. Wouldn't that be wild?"

"Yeah. It sure would," I said, my heart racing. There was something about this guy. Okay, not just something. *Everything.* He was gorgeous and athletic and passionate. And he seemed to like that I wasn't the makeup and nail polish type. Not that there was anything wrong with being a girly-girl. If that's what made you feel good about yourself, then I say doll yourself up and apologize to no one. That just wasn't me.

Kyle looked at me with sheer, sizzling lust; I could see he liked me just fine the way I was. I already found myself wondering what he might look like naked, and I sure liked what I saw in my mind's eye. Star athletes like Kyle probably considered bringing a woman to screaming orgasm a huge win, and dear God did I want to play that game with him.

"Wanna grab some dinner after practice?" he asked.

"I would love it," I said, tingling all over.

They say when you meet the right guy, you just *know.* And that's how I felt about Kyle right away, even though I barely knew him.

I guess we'd just have to start with dinner and see what happened next.

4

———————

MATT

(Six Years Later)

Losing my nerve that day in the spring of my junior year of college had turned out to be the biggest regret of my life. For all I knew, Julia might have gently rebuffed me, saying we could never be more than friends. That would have been gut-wrenching, but at least I would have known how she felt. I could have moved on with my life.

She wound up meeting another guy a few measly hours after I chickened out during our lunch together and now, six years later, she was still with him.

I stared at my reflection in the mirror as I buttoned my dress shirt, preparing to go out to dinner. Julia and her stupid boyfriend had come back to Pennsylvania now that it was October and the baseball season was over, and I was going to meet up with the happy couple. Well, two happy couples. Jerry was bringing his boyfriend, Parker. Though I wasn't crazy about being the fifth wheel on this double date, it was always fun to hang out with my buddy.

I slipped my tie over my neck and tied the knot. It had been a while since I'd had the occasion to get dressed up, and it was nice to be home. During the baseball season, I lived in a luxury apartment not far from Old Bay Stadium. The rest of the year, I lived in my house in central Pennsylvania. The season had just ended a week ago, and I'd enjoyed being at home, decompressing and resting my sore muscles from the grueling 162-game schedule.

My place was huge, especially compared to my apartment in Baltimore. It had four bedrooms, a spacious living room area, and a huge kitchen with lots of stainless-steel appliances. Cooking was one of my favorite off-season hobbies, and I looked forward to getting back into it.

Slipping on my suit jacket, I did my best to mentally prepare for tonight's dinner. I hadn't seen Julia in more than a year. As always, I tried to convince myself this time would be different. That my heart wouldn't sink when I saw her. That being with her wouldn't stir up all the emotions that I worked so hard to suppress. Still, I knew there was no denying the truth.

I loved Julia Frederick, and I hated Kyle Nolan.

I stepped outside into the crisp, refreshing evening air, which was a pleasant change from the heat and humidity of the summer. I slid behind the wheel of my silver Lexus. It was the perfect vehicle for me. Luxurious and comfortable without being flashy. As a major leaguer, I earned a lot of money, but I never felt the need to show it off. I appreciated my wealth but saw no reason to rub it in people's faces.

During the ride to the restaurant, vivid memories of that horrible day flashed in my mind. Try as I might, I couldn't forget the way Julia had looked on the ballfield that day. It had been such a pleasant surprise to see her. She frequently came to my baseball games, but I'd never seen her come to practice before. I recalled watching her sift the dirt through her fingers and breathe in the smell of the grass. She loved the outdoors and was passionate about gardening and planting.

I also recall standing there, watching in horror as the team heartthrob chatted her up. Even I couldn't fault Julia for falling for his charms. Sure, Julia and I had the love of sports in common, but that was pretty much all we had. Kyle was everything I wasn't. The man oozed charisma and was the life of the party, just like Julia. He commanded attention when he walked into a room the same way Julia did. When the two of them were together, you couldn't help being drawn to them. They were chatty and excitable. In short, they were fun to be around.

What did I have to offer Julia? A somber, serious disposition. A barrel of laughs I was not. Letting out a deep sigh, I reminded myself that only her happiness truly mattered. And she *was* happy. I could see the way she smiled when she was with him. Even in my private fantasies, I found it hard to imagine her being happy with me. It hurt like hell to think that way, but there was no denying the truth. Julia was better off with Kyle than she ever would be with me.

When I arrived at Roberto's Ristorante, the four of them were already there at the hostess' stand waiting to be seated.

"Matt!" Julia exclaimed as she rushed toward me. As usual, she didn't give a damn about being too loud for a fancy restaurant. I admired her for it. Kyle, however, glanced around as if uncomfortable with the noise his girlfriend had made.

She wrapped her arms around me, and I closed my eyes, breathing in that familiar, outdoorsy scent. I'd always been grateful she never wore perfume to mask her unique and delightful fragrance. When she released me from her all too brief embrace, I eyed her up and down.

"You look wonderful, Julia," I said. My heart hammered in my chest as I gazed upon her. She wore dress slacks and a lovely green blouse. I couldn't recall ever seeing her wear a dress, no matter how fancy the occasion.

"So do you, you strapping stud of a man," she said, gently slapping my shoulders. "You look dapper as hell, Matt."

"Thanks," I said, reveling in her approval. I had a pretty good poker face these days when it came to hiding my emotions. Years of unrequited love will do that to a person. Thankfully, I was a far cry from the blushing virgin I'd been on that incredible night with her in South Beach. I had been with a lot of women since that first time in college. It wasn't hard to find women who were willing to have sex with you once they found out you were a pro ballplayer. Most of the time they were just one-night stands, but I really did want to settle down and get married someday. The trouble was, I could never seem to picture myself with anyone besides Julia.

"Hey, Big Shot," Jerry said with a grin. When I made it to the majors he called me Mr. Big Shot Baseball Player. It had gotten shortened to Big Shot over the years. It was kind of an ironic nickname I guess, since I wasn't the type to flaunt my success. I was semi-famous and got recognized in public sometimes, but only by people who followed baseball. Most of the time I was anonymous, which was fine by me.

I nodded a greeting to Jerry. Though he often shared his sister's mushy, touchy-feely enthusiasm when greeting friends, we saw each other all the time so he clearly felt no need to pull me into a hug.

"How's the teeth business?" I asked him. Jerry had done well after college, having gone to dental school. He was working hard to build his dental practice here in PA.

"It's good," Jerry said enthusiastically. "The office is growing fast, both with patients and adding more employees. Can't complain."

"Good deal," I said, then turned to Kyle. "Nice to see you," I lied as I shook his hand.

I supposed it was childish to hold a grudge after all this time, but it was a gut reaction whenever I laid eyes on the guy. It was hard to tell if I only disliked him because he had won the heart of the woman I loved or if I would have disliked him no matter what. He was nice enough I guess, but he had sort of a cocky way about him that rubbed me the wrong way. Still, I managed to be civil to him and not let on that I hated him with the heat of a thousand suns.

After greeting Jerry's boyfriend, Parker, with a genuinely enthusiastic handshake, the five of us made our way to our table. We ordered some drinks and settled into conversation. It was hard for me not to stare at Julia from across the table. I still thought about her every single day. Indulging in a quick glance her way, I noted that she looked more beautiful than ever. Her luscious brown hair cascaded in curly waves around her shoulders, and her hazel eyes shone as brightly as ever.

Time had done nothing to diminish my useless devotion to her.

Averting my gaze and sipping my wine, I struggled to gain control of my emotions.

She's smiling. She's happy. That's all that matters.

"So, how did the Batters do this year?" I asked Julia. She was still with that Triple-A team in Kentucky, though now she was the head groundskeeper. Since her early days as an intern, she'd been consistently promoted until she held the top groundskeeping job. I was so proud of her.

"They're getting better," Julia said with a laugh. "I know that's not saying much. Had three guys get called up, and I love seeing that."

Kyle winced slightly.

Good, I thought, then instantly had the moral sense to feel a little guilty for thinking it.

After all these years, Kyle was still in the minor leagues. He played for a team in South Carolina, and he and Julia somehow made the long-distance relationship work. Their physical distance helped me sleep better at night, to be sure. At least I didn't have to imagine them having wild, athletic sex every night when half the time they were in different states. I did hope Julia wasn't lonely, though.

Having played so many years in the minors really made me appreciate how good I had it now. Everything was better in the majors. The travel and accommodations were much easier and more luxurious, and the salary was incredible. Minor league life was tough. You were on the road just as much as in the majors but mostly on smelly, overcrowded buses. You stayed in cheap motels, often with two other guys in the room with you. I supposed I should feel sorry for Kyle. In college, he'd been the star pitcher. The one to watch. Now, all these years later, he was stuck in the minors.

But he had Julia.

I would trade all my success if it meant I could be with her. As far as I was concerned, Kyle was still the reigning champion at this table.

Jerry was a close second, what with his successful dental practice and the fact that he was crazy in love with Parker. I liked Parker and never minded when he hung out with me and Jerry. With his reddish-brown hair and light blue eyes, he had boyish looks as well as charm. A pleasant, upbeat person, Parker worked for a homeless youth charity. He absolutely adored Jerry. They were good together. Other than being jealous of their relationship, I was happy for them.

"The Bay Birds were looking good this year," Parker said charitably, making me smile.

"Well, we're getting *better* at least," I said. The Baltimore Bay Birds were in a rebuilding process that had been going on for years. For a while there—fortunately before my time with them—they'd been truly horrible. But we'd just called up two excellent starting pitchers from the minors, and slowly but surely things were improving. I enjoyed playing for Baltimore, and my teammates were like my brothers. We weathered tough losses together as a supportive unit, and that helped us forge a tight bond.

"That Brady Keaton is something else," Kyle said, admiration in his voice.

"Yeah, he is," I chuckled. Brady was one of my closest friends on the team. Talk about a big shot. He was the type of celebrity athlete who was so well-known that even people who didn't follow baseball knew who he was. He was quite a character, and he certainly enjoyed the attention that fame brought him. But he was also one hell of a ballplayer, and he had your back, no matter what. Though I'd been wary of Brady at first, given all the crazy media attention his presence brought to our team, we became fast friends. When I saw him tear up on Opening Day, I thought, *Oh yeah. This guy gets it.* Like me, he knew how lucky we were to be playing major league baseball.

"That guy's like my hero," Kyle continued. "He's got it all.

He's an All-Star, got the Silver Slugger Award, and he's got all those commercial endorsements. The man must be loaded."

"He is," I said, feeling a bit strange about discussing my friend's wealth. "Brady's a good guy."

"Is he still with that girl?" Julia asked.

Just then, our server brought our meals. After everyone had their food in front of them, I answered her question.

"Yeah, he's still with Lyric."

Brady had made headlines when it came to light that his live-in girlfriend—the one who had charmed everyone by having seemingly tamed the playboy athlete—wasn't really his girlfriend after all. More than anything in the world, Brady had wanted to play for his hometown team, the Baltimore Bay Birds. The owner had distrusted him due to his wild reputation as a drunken partier. At the time, Lyric was a flat-broke college student struggling to save money for medical school. She'd reluctantly agreed to Brady's crazy idea to pretend to be his girlfriend to show the Baltimore owner that he had settled down and changed his ways.

Their relationship had started out as fake, but their love was real. They'd fallen for each other during the months of pretending to be a couple, and they'd been together ever since. Kyle was right about one thing: Brady really did have it all. He was a rich, successful athlete who had landed the woman of his dreams. As far as I was concerned, it couldn't have happened to a better guy. I was thrilled for my friend.

"Such a romantic love story," Julia said with a smile. "So, Matt, is there anyone special in your life?"

It took everything I had not to scoff out loud at that loaded question. Poker face firmly in place, I said, "Nope."

Julia sighed, and Jerry shook his head sadly. They were

both well aware that some woman in college had destroyed my heart and that was why I had such a hard time finding anyone else. Though they knew about the girl I loved who didn't love me back, neither of them had any inkling that it was Julia.

"I know you don't believe it," Jerry said as he twirled a forkful of pasta, "but I know you're gonna meet the right person someday."

He told me that all the time, and no. I didn't believe it. I appreciated it all the same. Jerry knew how much I wanted to get married and have a family.

"Stranger things have happened, I suppose," I said after swallowing a bite of delicious, cheesy lasagna.

"Never thought it would happen to me, either," Parker said, eying me with compassion. "But it did."

I nodded, recalling the time when he, Jerry, and I were hanging out on Jerry's porch having a few beers. After pounding several on an empty stomach, Parker had become rather emotional. He'd spoken about how hard it was for him to come out, and how he'd worried he might never find someone he could spend the rest of his life with. And then he'd met Jerry. Tearing up, he'd said how much he loved him. I'm not great at handling my own emotions, let alone somebody else's, but it was still rather sweet. That's when I'd known he would always take good care of my best friend. He was a good guy, that Parker.

As much as I appreciated the support of my friends, I was starting to feel uncomfortable with this whole conversation. Two happy couples saying *Aww, don't worry. You'll find somebody!* was a tad embarrassing. I tried to think of a way to steer the conversation back to baseball or something else. *Anything* else, really.

"So, Matt," Julia began with a smile. "Kyle and I have some news to share."

My heart felt like it dropped down to my shoes. There were only two ways this could play out. Either they were getting married, or Julia was pregnant. I wasn't sure which one would hurt worse.

"Is that right?" I asked. *Poker face, poker face.*

I allowed my gaze to drift down to her left hand. And sure enough ...

"We're getting married!" Julia chirped excitedly.

"That's great news, you two," I managed to say calmly while my insides exploded. Lifting my glass, I said, "Congratulations."

All five of us clinked, and I downed the rest of my glass in one shot. My friends all knew I was not the effusive, excitable type, so if nothing else, nobody expected me to shoot out of my chair and hug the happy couple. My understated reaction surprised no one, as it was the same way I would react no matter who had announced their engagement.

Well, I would have been a lot more enthusiastic had it been Jerry and Parker getting married.

At times like this, I wished Jerry knew I was in love with his sister—he would have warned me about this blow in advance. He remained blissfully oblivious, which I supposed was for the best. I couldn't imagine how he would feel if he knew I'd had sex with Julia in college.

Not that any of that mattered now. The only man Julia would have sex with was her husband.

Her husband.

Eying my empty wineglass, I fantasized about the nearly full bottle of Jack Daniels on my kitchen counter. Tomorrow

I would face this new, horrible reality. Tonight was the time to make myself forget.

The rest of the dinner consisted of us discussing wedding plans, the nuptials slated for December of the following year, and me feeling like I wanted to die.

Good times.

5

———

JULIA

A few days after my dinner with Matt and my brother, I got a phone call that changed my life. My body trembled the whole time I was on the phone with the executive from the Baltimore Bay Birds. I couldn't stop shaking, even after we ended the call.

I got the job.

My dream job. I was gonna be the head groundskeeper for the Baltimore Bay Birds. Old Bay Stadium was known as the most beautiful ballpark in all of major league baseball, and I would have the privilege of taking care of it.

I had just gotten engaged and now this?

I didn't know what I had done to deserve this, but I was so happy and grateful I could scream. I actually did scream, but not too loud lest the neighbors think I was being murdered. More likely, they would think Kyle and I were having sex, which we'd been doing a lot of since we'd finally been reunited at the end of the baseball season.

I was tempted to call Kyle immediately, but I managed to resist the urge. It was much better to deliver this news in person. That way, I could see the look on his face when I told him my dream had come true. I loved how he never expected me to be the glamorous, girly type, and that he thought it was cool that I played in the dirt for a living. As much as he loved baseball, I knew he would understand what an honor it would be to work at Old Bay Stadium in particular.

It made me happy that I'd gotten this news during the off-season when Kyle and I were living together. It was wonderful to be home with him after being apart so much of the time. Strange to think we still wouldn't have much time together even when we were married. That was the life for a ballplayer's wife. You had no say in where your guy had to work. He went wherever he was offered a place to play, and right now, that place was South Carolina. Instead of working in Kentucky, I would be in Baltimore, which still wasn't within reasonable driving distance of where Kyle played ball.

Things weren't as hectic now as they were during the baseball season, but we were both still pretty busy. Though the minor leagues were still considered professional baseball, they didn't pay a whole lot. Kyle and I saved what money we could, but it wasn't much. Unlike major league baseball players, Kyle had to find another job during the off-season. So did I. He waited tables, and I worked in a hardware store.

At last, Kyle came home from his day shift at the restaurant looking exhausted. That was kind of perfect, since what better time to get good news than when you were having a bad day? I was so excited, I could barely contain myself. Kyle would be so proud of me.

"Kyle! Kyle! Oh my God, you won't believe it!" I said, rushing to the door to greet him.

"What? What?" he said, jumping up and down to playfully mock me.

"I got the job," I said, breathless with excitement.

"What? What job?" Kyle asked, looking confused.

"That job for the Baltimore Bay Birds that I said I had no way in hell of getting, that's what job." I had interviewed months ago, and I hadn't thought it went well. I didn't know why, I just felt like that Gary Devilbuss owner guy didn't like me. I knew I was highly qualified for the job. God knows I'd worked my ass off every day since I graduated. I could handle the position, but that hadn't meant I would get it.

"The head groundskeeper job?" he asked.

"Yes!" I yelled. "Can you believe it?"

"Wow, that's great, honey. Really, really great," he said, sounding underwhelmed.

Not exactly the reaction I had hoped for. I would have expected that kind of reaction from Matt. That guy never acted excited, but that didn't mean he didn't feel anything. He had a way of holding his tongue and keeping his emotions in check, and then once in a while he would let you know how he really felt. One time, his voice cracked ever-so-slightly when he told me how happy he was that Jerry had found Parker. That was a flood of emotion coming from a guy like Matt. Kyle was a lot more expressive about his feelings. Usually.

Which made me wonder what was going through his head. He was happy for me ... right?

I decided to just ask him point-blank, because his reaction hurt. If he had gotten the call instead of me, I would still have been jumping up and down.

"Aren't you happy for me?" I asked.

"Baby, baby, of course I am," he said, throwing his arms around me. Laughing, he said, "I'm just still processing the news, I guess. The Baltimore Bay Birds. Wow. Damn. Hey, you can work with Matt."

"I know. Won't that be amazing? And I also get to work with your hero."

"Oh yeah," Kyle said, his eyes lighting up. "You'll get to work with Brady Keaton. Impressive."

So far, he was way more impressed that I would work alongside famous baseball players than with my huge accomplishment. I guess it wasn't entirely his fault. As a man, he really had no clue how hard it was for a woman to land this kind of gig. But I knew. I knew what I'd been through all these years and how hard I'd worked to gain respect as a female in a male-driven sport.

I paused for a moment, giving him a chance to realize he was hurting me with his lackluster response to my earth-shattering news. He didn't say anything else.

"This means I'll be making a lot more money, you know. That might mean you never have to take another off-season job again and you can just focus on baseball," I told him.

"Hey, yeah," Kyle said, his face brightening.

My heart sank. That had been a test, and he'd failed miserably.

"So now you're excited," I said irritably. "Now that you see what's in it for you. More money and you might get to meet Brady Keaton."

"I didn't mean it like that," he said, finally having the good sense to look guilty for his reaction to my news.

"You have no idea how hard I worked for this."

"Julia," Kyle said, pulling me into his arms. "Of course I do. I don't know anybody who works as hard as you do. This is incredible. I'm sorry if I didn't seem excited enough. I'm just really worn down after a long day, and you took me by surprise."

Kyle smiled and shook his head in wonder. "Old Bay Stadium. Of all places. That is *amazing*."

"Right?" I said, my spirits lifting again at last.

"Look at you, you rising star. I'm so proud of you, baby. So proud."

Kyle gazed into my eyes and smiled, showing off those dimples I adored. And suddenly everything was right again in my world. I was gonna marry my best friend next year, and now I had my dream job on top of it.

"We should go out and celebrate. How about Marley's?"

I grimaced inwardly. That place was a dive, but Kyle liked it for some reason. I was kinda surprised he'd suggested it since he knew I wasn't exactly a fan.

"Uh, how about the Brew Barn?" I asked.

"Sure. We can do that."

The Brew Barn—an old barn that had been converted into a bar and restaurant—was my favorite local place to drink and unwind.

Life was good. So, so good.

I smiled as we headed out the door, already dreaming about my job. Chuckling to myself, I decided to tell Jerry about the Bay Birds position and then swear him to secrecy.

I couldn't wait to surprise Matt when he showed up at Old Bay Stadium to start the new season.

6

MATT

A familiar thrill rippled through my body as I unpacked my gym bag and started arranging my things in my clubhouse locker. This was only my third year playing in the majors, and I hoped it would always feel this way. We'd gotten back from spring training in Florida a few days ago, and now we would practice at Old Bay Stadium for a few days. Then, after a few exhibition games, it would be Opening Day. The off-season had been relaxing, but I was more than ready to get back to playing ball. I eagerly anticipated playing the game I loved in front of a crowd of loyal, hometown fans.

The clubhouse scent was fresh right now—a mix of cleanser and leather from the balls, gloves, and other equipment. That wouldn't last long, though. After the season really got going, it would smell of sweat, dirty laundry, and stale deodorant spray. I rather liked that smell. It was the scent of baseball.

I heard rapid, heavy footsteps behind me. I didn't have to turn around to know who it was. Brady Keaton. The guy was huge, tall and muscular, and he always made an entrance everywhere he went. Thanks to his deep brown eyes, dark brown hair, and impressive physique, he'd graced the covers of all sorts of magazines from Sports Illustrated to GQ.

"Hey, man," I said, smiling at him. "So? How did it go?"

I could tell how it had gone from the grin on his face.

"She said yes," Brady said with a boyish grin.

"I had no doubts she would," I told him, clapping him on the shoulder.

Brady's weekend plans had included proposing to his longtime girlfriend. Lyric was a terrific woman, and she was good for him. Though I hadn't known Brady during his wilder days, I'd heard stories. Our star pitcher, Angel Jimenez, knew him from way back. Said he was always a ladies' man back in the minors but was pretty well-behaved until he hit the majors. Then he'd become quite a partier, drinking heavily and stirring up trouble. Though Lyric had never tried to change him, loving her did change him. Brady was still a lot of fun, but no longer a danger to himself or others.

"Did she cry?" I asked.

Brady chuckled. "Of course she did."

"Did you cry?"

His lip quavered, and he quickly wiped an imaginary tear from his eye. "No. Shut up. *You're* crying."

I laughed. "You set a date?"

"Yeah. The only time we can get married anytime soon. During the All-Star break in July. Any other time she'll be in school or I'll be playing ball."

"Makes sense."

Lyric attended Johns Hopkins University here in Baltimore, and it was a ton of work. It would have been tough to try to have a wedding during all that madness. Still, July was just four short months away.

"So you better not make the All-Star team this year," Brady said sternly. "Or you can't be in the wedding."

I smiled, both at his casual invitation to be in his wedding and the idea that I could make the All-Star team. I was a good ballplayer, but I wasn't *that* good.

"The bigger worry is *you* making the team, Hot Stuff."

Brady shrugged. "If I do, I'll just have to miss it this year."

He had already made the team twice, so it was a distinct possibility he would get chosen. The man was passionate about baseball, and I knew it would still mean a lot to him no matter how many times he was selected as an All-Star. But I knew he loved Lyric more.

"Ready to do this thing?" he asked, grinning and gesturing toward the door.

"More than ready," I said.

We were like little kids ready to get out on the field at recess. Grabbing our gear, we walked through the clubhouse and out to the dugout.

When Brady had joined the team, we'd bonded quickly over our love for baseball. He'd later confessed that he thought I might be a jerk when we first met. Unfortunately, I have that effect on people sometimes. Classic case of resting bitch face, I supposed. Once people got to know me, they figured out I was just quiet and that I wasn't silently judging them. With Brady as shortstop and me playing second base, it was critical that we worked well together to turn double plays. Fortunately, we got along beautifully.

We set our bags down on the dugout bench and drew in deep breaths as we looked out onto the field. There was nothing like that first moment back at Old Bay Stadium after weeks of playing on smaller fields in Florida. Brady had a deep reverence for his hometown stadium and never took a moment here for granted. I, too, was honored to play for the Bay Birds and grateful to be in the major leagues. So many players would never get this chance.

It also didn't hurt that we happened to play in one of the most beautiful parks in the majors. After Old Bay Stadium was built, many other ballparks copied a lot of the design. The field was lush and beautiful, ready for a season's worth of punishment. With only a slight chill in the early spring air, it was a perfect day to play ball.

Dear God, I love this game.

Gazing out at the ballfield on a picture-perfect day naturally made me think of Julia, knowing she would appreciate this moment as much as I did. She, of all people, understood how much work it took to keep the grass and infield in perfect playing shape.

I thought I saw her walking toward me on the field, which wasn't unusual for me. I thought of her so often that I'd lost count of how many times I'd seen her in places I knew she could not possibly be. My eyes had even played tricks on me during my summer trip to London, when I knew for sure she was home, working in Pennsylvania. In my mind and heart, Julia was everywhere.

But this time was different.

This time it *was* Julia Frederick, the love of my life, walking toward me on the field.

"Hey, you okay, buddy?" Brady asked. I barely registered the sound of his voice.

Staring at the familiar curly hair pulled back in a ponytail under a Baltimore Bay Birds baseball cap, my mind struggled to register the truth.

"Matt? Dude!" Brady said, sounding genuinely concerned.

I was usually good at keeping my face neutral in any

situation, especially where Julia was concerned. I'd had years of experience pretending she was just a friend to me. This time, I'd had no warning, no inkling that I'd have any chance of seeing her anytime soon.

Julia's face broke into a beautiful if mischievous smile when she got closer to me.

Get it together.

Shaking my head and smiling, I asked, "What in the world are you doing here?"

I swallowed hard, doing my best to calm my jackhammering heartbeat. Over the years I'd gotten used to the dull ache of loving a woman who would never love me back. A girl with a killer smile and hazel eyes that lit up the whole world. One who was set to marry another. The ache was a constant companion, but the sharp, painful shock of seeing her with no warning threw me completely off guard.

"I work here, Matt," Julia said with a burst of laughter. "You have no idea how hard it was to keep it a secret from you, but I wanted so much to surprise you."

"You ... work here?"

"Yeah," she said, breathless with excitement. "I'm the head groundskeeper."

"That's great," Brady said. I'd totally forgotten he was there. I glanced over at him, and he shot me a *what in the hell is your problem?* look. He'd never seen me rattled like this. I could only pray that I had fixed my face before Julia got a good look at my initial reaction to seeing her.

My head spun as I considered the gravity of the situation. Julia was working here. At Old Bay Stadium. I would see her every day.

I had no idea how in the hell I would survive having her around all the time.

"Matt?" Her expression fell. "Aren't you happy?"

Forget your feelings, you selfish prick. This is her dream job, and nobody deserves it more than she does.

"Of course I am," I said, laughing softly. "I'm sorry. I was just so surprised. You know how it is when you see some-body out of context and you can't quite figure out what's going on?"

"Yeah," Julia said. Her smile was back, as was the light in those hazel eyes.

"I can't even begin to tell you how proud I am of you. Just a few years ago you were an intern. And look at you now."

At last, the surge of adrenaline began to subside. More in control, my familiar instinct of emotional deception kicked in.

"My God, Julia. Of all the parks in baseball where you could be working ..."

You had to walk into mine.

"... you get to work in the most beautiful one of them all."

"Ain't that the truth," Brady said with a wide grin.

"I know," Julia whispered. "I just can't believe it."

I followed her gaze as it swept across the luscious ball-park, just as Brady and I had admired it when we'd first walked out here.

"No wonder it looks especially beautiful today," I said. "I might have known this was your handiwork. Congratula-tions, girl."

"Thanks, Matt," she said, grabbing me and pulling me into a hug.

I breathed in deeply, unsure if the smell of grass and dirt was from the ground or from her. It didn't matter. It was the scent of Julia Frederick.

I held her for as long as possible. Though I wasn't the

huggy, touchy-feely type, I *always* longed to touch her. I would take whatever physical affection I could get.

When she finally let go, I had to stifle a groan and fight the urge to grab her and hold her close.

She radiated excitement about her job. I would just have to deal with the emotional fallout that would come from working with her. The only thing that mattered was she had landed the job of her dreams.

"I'm Brady Keaton, by the way," Brady said, offering his hand to her.

"Oh God. I'm so sorry. Brady, this is Julia Frederick. We grew up together."

"Frederick," he said, his brow furrowing for a moment. "Oh, you must be Jerry's sister."

"Right, that's me," she said with a smile.

"Oh cool," Brady said. "Yeah, me and Matt have gone out with your brother a few times when he's been in town to catch a game or two. Nice guy."

Julia nodded and smiled. "Yeah, he is. Well, I better go," she said, looking around at the field. "Still lots of work to be done before Opening Day. Nice to meet you, Brady."

"Likewise," he said with a grin.

"I'll be seein' you around, Matt," Julia said with a laugh, utterly clueless that her proximity spelled disaster for me.

Brady and I stood and watched her walk across the field.

Once she was safely out of earshot, Brady asked, "What the hell was that?"

"What the hell was what?" I asked, knowing damn well what he was talking about. As much as I hoped he would just drop it, I knew my friend better than that.

"You looked like you saw a ghost when you first saw that girl," he said.

I refused to turn toward Brady, but I could feel his eyes boring into me.

"It's like I said, it was just strange to see her out of context. Last I heard, she was still working in Kentucky. I had no idea she was anywhere near here. Just took me by surprise."

"You got a history with Julia, don't you?"

I just gave her my virginity and my heart, that's all.

"No. We've never dated or anything."

"But you have a thing for her," he said, still staring at me.

"Drop it, Brady."

He kept silent for a moment.

"Well, maybe nothing's happened between you two before, but now that she's working here ..."

"I said *drop it.*" It took a lot to get me riled up, but I wasn't made of stone. Seeing Julia had shoved me badly off-kilter, and the last thing I needed was to talk about it.

"Matt, I'm just sayin'—"

"She's engaged," I snapped.

Brady let out a deep breath. "Oh. Dude, I'm really sorry. That sucks."

I nodded wordlessly.

And just like that, in a matter of minutes, Brady had figured out what nobody else ever had. I was in love with Julia Frederick. Scary how letting my mask slip even for a few seconds had given me away.

I wasn't worried, though. Brady could be a tad impulsive and even immature at times, but he was like a brother to me. He was a fiercely loyal friend, and I knew he would never breathe a word about this to anyone. In an odd way, I felt slightly relieved that *somebody* finally knew about my feelings for Julia. I would have to keep my poker face on constantly from now on around here, but at least Brady would understand the torture I was going through. When Julia inevitably showed up with Kyle in tow, Brady would be aware of how hard it was on me.

I headed over toward the plate, hoping that beating the shit out of a baseball or two would relieve some of my tension.

7

JULIA

Dear God in Heaven, did I love this job.

I arrived at the park early in the morning, reveling in the quiet that came before the madness of the day. Surveying the lush grass of the field and admiring the freshly hosed-down infield dirt, I could barely contain my excitement. After me and my crew had busted our asses all spring to get this gorgeous place ready, Opening Day was only a few days away. It was all I could do not to go skipping down the warning track.

Sometimes I actually did that. But only super early in the morning before anybody else got there. As much as I'd loved working on the field with the Kentucky Mad Batters, this was on a whole other level.

As the day wore on, the players began to arrive for batting practice, and the air crackled with excitement. It had been a long winter, and everybody was eager to get back to baseball. We had an exhibition game today, which meant the stands would be filled with fans. The game didn't count, of course. It was a dry run before the official season kicked off, and I was grateful for the time to work out any kinks before Opening Day.

I stood back to watch the guys at batting practice. I'd gotten pretty attached to the players on the Mad Batters team, and I looked forward to getting to know the players here. It helped that I already knew Matt, and Brady seemed very cool, too. I'd also met Angel Jimenez, a super nice guy who couldn't stop showing me pictures of his kid. He was adorable.

I watched Brady launch a few balls out into the bleachers. Some fans had arrived early to watch batting practice, and they cheered like mad every time Brady smacked the ball hard. Shivers of excitement went through me. If I was having this much fun now, what would the real season be like?

How is this my life?

I shook my head in wonder, taking it all in and wanting to relish every moment.

"Way to go, Crush!" yelled a woman sitting in the first row behind the Bay Bird's dugout. Brady jogged over, and the woman got up from her seat. When he leaned over the railing of the stadium to kiss her, I realized she must be the famous Lyric Rivers I'd heard about. Now that I got a closer look, I did recognize her from pictures in the media.

Brady caught my eye and smiled. He motioned me over.

"Hey, Julia, I'd like you to meet my fiancée, Lyric."

I reached over to shake her hand. "Hi, Lyric. Great to meet you."

"Julia is the new head groundskeeper here," Brady said.

"Oh yeah, I heard about you. I read that you're only the second woman to hold this job in the majors, right?" she asked with a sweet smile. Lyric had the prettiest blue eyes

I'd ever seen. With her dark hair and pale skin, she reminded me of Snow White.

"Yep, that's right."

"Well, it'll be nice to get some more estrogen around here," Lyric said, and I laughed.

"Julia grew up with Matt Jovey," Brady said.

"Get outta here. That's so funny," she said. "Matt's great."

"Yeah, he sure is. My twin brother, Jerry, is his best friend. The three of us used to play together when we were kids."

"That is so cool," Lyric said. "Such a small world."

"I didn't even tell Matt when I got the job. I wanted to surprise him," I said, giggling when I remembered the look on Matt's face when I came walking up to him. It was tough to get a rise out of that man, and for once I had actually done it.

"Oh, he was surprised all right," Brady said.

"The field looks fabulous," Lyric said, gazing out at the park. "I know how hard you guys work on it. Seen your crew out here at all hours of the day and night."

"Yeah, it's a tough job, but I couldn't love it any more," I said.

"I know what you mean."

"I'm sure you do. You're in medical school, right? That must be a killer." I'd had enough trouble sitting still in class just getting my associate's degree. I couldn't begin to imagine the stamina it took to survive four years of college and then medical school.

"Oh, it can be, for sure," she said wearily. "But I know it'll all be worth it. *Someday.*"

"Yeah, it will," I said.

Shaking her head, Lyric said, "I can't imagine how hard

you must have worked to get here, Julia. It's such a male-dominated field, no pun intended."

"You got that right," I said. Things were improving, but it had been a struggle to get some of the guys I worked with to take me seriously. Helped that I was the boss now. My crew here at Old Bay Stadium was great, thank goodness. Still, they knew I had the power to fire them if they refused to do their jobs properly. Granted, that was a last resort, but I wasn't afraid to cut somebody loose if they got too big for their britches. "I can't imagine it's any easier in the medical world."

"Has its challenges to be sure," she said.

"Well, if it helps, you got me in your corner. Feel free to come bitch to me anytime."

"I just might take you up on that," Lyric said.

"Men!" Brady huffed with exaggeration.

Lyric laughed, gazing at him with adoration. "They're not all bad. I snagged a good one."

"Me too," I said, holding up my left hand just as Matt happened to walk over to us. He'd just finished his turn at batting practice. "You're a good one too, Matt," I said, slinging my arm around his neck. It made me so happy to be working with him. I'd missed hanging out with him on a regular basis ever since I graduated from college.

"Oh, I'm aware," Lyric said with a smile. "He and Brady are good friends, so we hang out with Matt all the time."

"Then you know he's a swingin' single," I said with a wink. "Just in case you know of anybody who might be good for him."

"Believe me, I would love to set him up with somebody, but he never lets me," Lyric said.

"Same here," I said. "Stubborn jackass."

Matt just shrugged. I wished he could somehow get over

that woman who'd broken his heart in college. I truly believed he could be happy with somebody else if he just gave new love a chance.

"So tell me about your fiancé," Lyric said.

I smiled. "Kyle's a baseball player too, actually. Plays in the minors right now, and it's tough being away from him all the time. He's in South Carolina."

"Oh wow, that must be hard," Lyric said, her eyes filled with sympathy. "So tell me. How did he propose?"

"Oh, it was really sweet. Super romantic. He proposed over wine and a candlelit dinner in a fancy restaurant."

"He did?" Matt asked, sounding surprised.

"Yeah, why?"

Shrugging, he said, "I don't know. That sounds nice, I guess. But it's not exactly your style."

I sighed. Matt knew me so well.

"You're right. Oh, this is gonna sound so terrible ... so ungrateful ... but I admit, I was kind of disappointed."

I was surprised at the relief I felt saying those words out loud. Everybody *oohed* and *aahed* when I told them Kyle proposed by slipping the ring into my wineglass as a surprise. And it *was* sweet. And yet ...

"Proposing in the middle of a baseball field would have made more sense," Matt grumbled, making me smile. It was endearing how annoyed he seemed on my behalf.

"Yeah. You're right."

"Really?" Lyric asked, eyes wide. "Dear God, that would have given me an anxiety attack."

Brady chuckled. "Yeah, it sure would have. I knew better than to pull a stunt like that."

"Julia would have loved it," Matt said, still sounding irritable. "She loves sports, especially baseball. She played softball all through high school and college. Her happy place is outside on the playing field. And she loves getting attention as much as she loves showering attention on other people."

"I can understand that," Lyric said. "I mean, it's definitely not for me, but I get it. You see those scoreboard proposals a lot, and that's great as long as it's what's right for the couple."

My heart sank. I still felt horribly ungrateful, but I had to admit that Kyle's proposal bothered me. I wasn't a fancy restaurant type of person. And I felt like he should have known that. A wedding proposal was a once-in-a-lifetime opportunity, and I'd dreamed of being proposed to publicly and having people burst into applause around us, celebrating our love with us. I guess it was petty of me, but the truth was I'd fantasized more about the proposal than my actual wedding. Oh well. The marriage was the most important thing, not all the pomp and circumstance surrounding the ceremonial stuff. I loved Kyle, and that was all that mattered.

"So how did Brady propose?" I asked, wanting to change the subject from my engagement.

"Oh, it's gonna sound so lame," Brady lamented.

"No, not at all," Lyric said, reaching over to grab his hand and squeeze it before letting go. "It was simple and lovely and absolutely *perfect*. See, we have such crazy schedules, especially during the baseball season. He's often out late at night at the ballpark or on the road with the team, and I'm usually overwhelmed with medical school. Our way of reconnecting is to sit together on the couch with a couple of beers and cuddle and watch TV."

"That sounds really sweet," I said with a smile. "Simple, yet intimate."

"It's really nice," she said, smiling at Brady. "Gives us a chance to get away from the crowds and the media and all of that, and just be *us*. And then one night when we were just chilling out on the couch as usual, he got down on one knee ...”

Lyric's pretty blue eyes filled with tears.

“And it was so utterly perfect. It wasn't for the cameras or the media. It was just for me ... for us. What made it perfect was Brady understood exactly what was right for me. He loves getting lots of attention, but he knows I don't.”

I knew by the way she looked at Brady that they would be happy together for the rest of their lives.

Just like me and Kyle. So his proposal wasn't perfect. Nobody was perfect. I sure as hell wasn't, and no doubt there were lots of things I'd done to hurt or annoy him without even knowing it.

“That's really lovely, Brady,” I said, punching him lightly on the shoulder. “Good job.”

“Thanks,” he said with a laugh. “I do what I can.”

“Have you set a date for your wedding?” Lyric asked.

“Yeah, it's in December,” I said. “That works for *our* crazy baseball schedules. Besides, I just love Christmastime so it should be really fun.”

“That does sound fun. Ours is gonna be kind of a whirl-wind to plan,” Lyric said, sounding slightly anxious. “It's this July, during the All-Star break. Timing's a bit tight, but with me in school and all that, it's gonna be tough for a while yet. And I just hated the idea of putting it off.”

Lyric gazed over at Brady again and smiled. He smiled, too, and the look between them was like they were communicating in a secret language. They had something so sweet, so intimate about them. You could tell they were connected body, heart, and soul and were eager to make that connection legal, publicly pledging their love in marriage.

I felt the same about Kyle. Yep. No doubt about it.

8

———

MATT

I stepped up to the plate at batting practice a few hours before the Opening Day ceremonies began. I grunted as I swung hard and missed the ball. It was not a good sign when you couldn't connect with the ball during batting practice. Despite hitting well during spring training in Florida, I'd been terrible since we got back to Baltimore.

And I was pretty sure I knew why.

Since enduring the discussion about Kyle proposing to Julia, I'd done my best to avoid being around her. I knew I was right when I'd said his proposal was all wrong for her, but afterward, I felt bad about saying it out loud. It wasn't right for me to trash Kyle and cast doubt on the way he'd asked Julia to marry him. Though I was no fan of Kyle's, that was my issue and not his. It was not his fault that he was lucky enough to have won Julia's heart. She loved him, and she was going to marry him in December. Julia deserved to be happy, even if it wouldn't be with me.

"You okay?" Brady asked me when I returned to the dugout after mangling batting practice.

"Yep. Just fine."

He knew I wasn't fine, but he didn't say it. I had to get a mental and emotional grip on myself if I didn't want this season to be a complete disaster. Somehow, I needed to deal with Julia's presence. It was so much easier when she'd lived in another state.

When the Opening Day ceremonies began, I tried to focus on baseball and not my broken heart. Standing there in uniform next to my teammates was an honor as always, and I took a moment to appreciate my good fortune.

I was playing major league baseball in the most beautiful ballpark in the sport. I would do well to never forget how lucky I was to be here. Plenty of days in college and in the minors, I'd feared I wouldn't make it this far. I'd never needed my computer science degree, and for that I was deeply grateful.

My heart swelled with pride when I removed my cap and placed it over my heart as the national anthem began to play. It was the first of 162 times I would hear it during the season. Damn, it felt good to be back on the field.

Surveying the ballfield, the opposing team, and my own team, my eyes landed on my beloved Julia's face. As I watched her wipe a tear from her eye, all the emotions I'd tried to suppress came rushing back. The picture of calm on the outside, I was still the same lovesick boy I'd been back in college. I'd been completely off-kilter since Julia had shocked me by showing up in the place where I'd least expected her.

If I wasn't over Julia Frederick by now, I never would be.

My mind was a mess, and I couldn't see the ball well at all. The best I could manage during the game was a walk, striking out twice and then popping out for my final at bat of the game.

The Bay Birds won in a close game with a final score of

3-2. Throughout the game, I couldn't help watching the grounds crew as they smoothed out the field and kept everything in pristine playing condition. I figured I'd be able to resist that temptation after a while. Having Julia as head groundskeeper at Old Bay Stadium was new. Eventually, I would get used to her presence.

I had to. Otherwise, my entire career would be screwed.

As per our Opening Day tradition, several of us players headed over to Brady's basement bar to have a few drinks to toast the new season. Brady was such a superstar that going out to a public bar along with a bunch of other Bay Birds attracted too much attention. Being tucked away at his enormous house not far from the stadium afforded us all a chance to unwind with our significant others. Well, those of us who had them, anyway.

"Hey," Brady said from his place behind the bar. He loved bartending for his friends.

I took a seat on the stool right in front of him and he slid a frosty mug of beer my way.

Leaning in close, he said, "Dude, I'm really sorry, but Julia's gonna be here."

My heart sank to the pit of my stomach—an all too familiar feeling these days.

"Oh." I took a healthy sip of beer.

"Lyric invited her. She doesn't know that you're, you know ..."

In love with Julia.

"I know. I get it. It's cool," I said. Brady looked doubtful. "I gotta get used to being around her."

"You're really rattled, aren't you?" he said, dark eyes full of concern. Brady was rarely this serious, but he knew how much baseball meant to me and that Julia's presence was the reason for my abysmal performance today.

"Yeah. I am." I took another gulp of beer. "But I just gotta deal with it. Gonna be a long season otherwise."

"I get it, you know," he said quietly. "I just ... I don't know what I would do if Lyric was engaged to somebody else."

I nodded, feeling relieved all over again to have somebody in my corner. I'd carried this burden my whole life without anybody knowing. Well, nobody knew the specifics. Julia and Jerry knew I'd been burned badly by love, but they had no idea how close the deadly flame was.

"Ohhh," Brady said, his eyes lighting up.

"Oh, what?" I asked.

"She was the one. The one in college who broke your heart."

I chuckled softly. It was like he'd been reading my mind. Not long after he joined the team, Brady invited me over to his place for a few drinks. I'd had a few too many that night and wound up confessing my feelings for a girl I'd known in college. It was rather cool of him to remember that after all this time.

"Yeah."

"*Shit,*" Brady said, probably realizing all over again how screwed I was.

The door swung open behind me, and I could tell it was Julia by the grim look on Brady's face.

"Poker face, man. Poker face," I said sternly.

"Right," Brady said, brightening up immediately. "What's your pleasure, Julia?"

Julia slung her arm around my neck and kissed my cheek. Brady winced but recovered quickly.

"A shot. Of anything. Don't care what."

"Comin' right up," Brady said. He poured her a drink in a shot glass and slid it toward her.

After downing it in one gulp, she set the glass down on

the bar. "Another!"

"You sure?" Brady asked.

"She can handle it," I told him. "Believe me."

Laughing, Brady said, "Okay. I'll hook you up."

Julia downed the next shot just as quickly. She let out a deep, satisfied sigh. "That's how I get my party started."

She held up her hand to show Brady she was good for now. He nodded and then turned to greet more guests who were vying for his attention.

Though nobody was likely to get trashed on this Thursday night, it was safe to let loose a little. We had an off-day already tomorrow. They had planned it that way just in case the original Opening Day got rained out. After that, it would be another week or so until we got a day off.

"So how was your first day?" I asked Julia. "Was it everything you expected?"

"All that and so much more," she said, her hazel eyes filled with joy and excitement. Seeing her happy made my own pain well worth it. Julia belonged at Old Bay Stadium every bit as much as I did. In spite of everything, I was glad she was here. "I just can't even believe that I work there, you know what I mean?"

"Yes. I know exactly what you mean. And if you're anything like me, that feeling doesn't go away. I still get chills every Opening Day."

"That's wonderful, Matt," she said, gazing at me with such fondness that it nearly took my breath away. Julia did love me. As a friend, and that would simply have to be enough.

Since she was my good friend, I knew I could confide in her about anything. Well, *almost* anything.

"Feels so good to be playing again, but I'm a little worried."

"About what?" Julia asked with concern.

"About not hitting. I know it's only the first game and all, but I'm struggling already. It's weird because I did pretty well during spring training. And then it's like all of a sudden I'm not seeing the ball. Not connecting." I shrugged as if I had no idea what the problem might be.

"That's tough," she said. "Makes you feel off balance."

"Yes. Exactly."

Nodding, Julia said, "I've seen guys on the Mad Batters go through that, and I know how hard it can be. Kyle's gone through tough times too, though he doesn't worry so much about batting as a pitcher. If he winds up in the American League, batting won't be an issue at all. But I've seen how hard it can be to go through a slump. This may not even be a slump. It's only the first day, and the opposing pitcher was really good."

Wordlessly, Brady slid another beer my way the instant my first one was empty. Nodding my thanks to him, I turned back to Julia.

"Yeah, I guess he was."

"Not like it was a blowout and everybody else was teeing off the guy. Bay Birds scored three runs total after all."

"True," I said. Both the beer and Julia's cheerful words made me feel better. Sitting here and talking with her felt like old times, but in a good way. She was a good friend to me—to everybody, really—and it was in her nature to build people up. Of course, that was one of the things I loved about her.

Sighing deeply, I picked up my mug and took a drink.

Attributing my weary sigh to my baseball woes and not unrequited love, she put a supportive hand on my shoulder.

"It's gonna get better, Matt. You'll see."

God, I hope so.

9

JULIA

Opening Day had been beyond incredible, and I'd taken in every moment. The swirling smells of food, grass, dirt, and sunscreen—all those familiar scents that blended together on a perfect day for baseball. The stands had been packed, as I knew they would be on the first day after months with no baseball. I had to be realistic, though. Since the Baltimore Bay Birds weren't exactly the greatest team, over time the crowds would thin if they didn't play well. Still, I was thrilled to be a part of the rebuilding of the team, and I dreamed they would make it to the World Series during what I hoped would be my lifetime career in Baltimore. There was just nowhere else I wanted to be.

But there was a huge downside. It hurt like hell that Kyle hadn't been with me to share in this amazing day. I knew he would have been here if he could, but his baseball season was just starting up as well. My heart ached that I couldn't be there to cheer him on for his Opening Day, either. This long-distance stuff was tough. My fondest hope was that not only would Kyle get called up to the majors, but that he could play for the Baltimore Bay Birds. Seeing as his current team was the minor league affiliate for the Florida Devils, that was pretty unlikely.

I had the luxury of sleeping in today, and I was grateful to wake up well-rested. Even on off-days for the boys, I had work to do at the ballpark, but it was less urgent than on game days. I'd head to Old Bay Stadium in a little while, but I wanted to do a video call with Kyle first. At 11am, I figured it was late enough not to wake him but early enough that he wouldn't be at the ballpark yet for his day game.

Settling in at my kitchen counter, I opened my laptop. I had sublet a tiny one-bedroom apartment in Baltimore for the season. Poor Kyle was stuck in a similar situation in South Carolina, and yet we still had to pay rent on our apartment in Pennsylvania until our lease was up. After that, we'd probably find a bigger apartment around here since my job was relatively stable. Unlike Kyle, it wasn't likely I'd be sent to work for another team for a while, if ever. We couldn't even think of buying a house right now. Not only could we not afford it, we never knew when or if Kyle would get called up to the majors.

"Hey baby," Kyle said with a grin.

My heart soared like it always did when I saw him. How I loved that mischievous, dimpled smile that had won me over so many years ago. I reached out and touched the screen, wishing I could hold him.

"I miss you so much," I said. The first few days of a new baseball season were always the hardest. After spending all of fall and winter together, it was tough to get used to being apart.

"I miss you too," he said.

"You doing okay?"

"Yeah, I'm okay. Team's up 3-0 for the season, so off to a great start."

"You're pitching today, right?"

"Yep. Playin' Cleveland."

"Cool," I said. "Since it's an afternoon start, maybe we'll have time to talk again after the game."

Kyle shrugged. "Maybe."

I paused for a moment, waiting for him to ask me how Opening Day went.

"I've always pitched well against this team, so I'm not too worried about it," he said. "Really been perfecting my cutter, so that's cool."

"Uh-huh," I managed to say.

I couldn't believe he still hadn't asked about my big day. As much as I'd tried not to think about it, it really hurt that he hadn't called yesterday or even texted to see how the game went. Reaching the major leagues as head groundskeeper was my lifelong dream. It was my first major league game. Opening Day for the Baltimore Bay Birds, for God's sake. There had been a ton of pressure on me to make sure everything went smoothly. It was as if he'd forgotten what was going on in my life altogether.

I nodded and listened patiently while Kyle discussed the starting lineup of the opposing team and how he planned to handle each guy. He'd always said that one of the things he loved about me was my thorough knowledge of baseball. He could discuss the intricacies of the sport with me. That was all well and good, but I wished he would return the favor when it came to things that were important to me. I didn't expect him to understand the details of grass seed and dirt science or anything, but how could he not even ask how my first day felt?

"So how was yesterday?" Kyle asked at last, but only after

he'd finished describing his battle plan for today's game in minute detail.

I thought for a moment about how to respond. The truth was that the day had been utterly exhilarating from start to finish. Frightening, exciting, thrilling, and emotional to the point where I teared up during the national anthem and not just out of patriotism. Opening Day at Old Bay Stadium had been everything I had dreamed of and so much more. As much as I'd hoped with all my heart to work in the major leagues someday, a big part of me thought it would never happen. And yet somehow it had.

I had all those words on the tip of my tongue, ready to come spilling out, but it felt like a waste of energy and emotion to share those feelings with someone who didn't seem all that interested.

"It was amazing," I finally said. A vast understatement, but there it was.

"That's good," he said with a smile. I waited for him to ask me for details. "Glad you had nice weather for it."

"Yeah. Me too."

"So how do you think the Baltimore Bay Birds will do this year?" he asked.

Trying to ignore the crushing disappointment I felt, I said, "Hard to say. They're still in a rebuilding period, so it's highly unlikely that they'll make the playoffs or anything this year. Still, the fans are loyal and that makes it a lot of fun. Baseball is big in Baltimore, and being around all the crowds and excitement is a blast. And of course, the stadium is so beautiful. It's such an honor to work there."

"Yeah, them Birds have been pretty bad these last couple of years. Hope the rebuilding efforts work for their sake."

My frustration mounted, as I couldn't seem to steer the conversation back to my part in the game of baseball.

"Matt sure had a rough outing," Kyle said, shaking his head and laughing. "Makes me feel better that I'm not the only one who struggled."

That crack pissed me off. Matt was my friend, and he was clearly in pain last night as he spoke about his batting struggles.

"That's not very nice of you, Kyle. Matt's a good guy. Why would you be happy he's having a hard time?"

"I'm not happy, Julia. I'm just sayin' I'm kinda sick and tired of being one of the older guys on my team and still trapped in the minors," he grumbled.

That quelled my anger a little. I knew how hard it was for Kyle to still be a minor leaguer. Unlike most other careers, ballplayers had a relatively short shelf life. He had some time yet, but one day he would be too old to be sent up to the majors. The harsh truth was that a lot of minor leaguers simply didn't make it. It was scary that unlike Matt, Kyle really had no Plan B. Sometimes I wondered if it had ever occurred to Kyle that he might not have a successful baseball career.

"So I hung out with some of the players last night at Brady Keaton's house," I said, knowing that would get his attention.

"No shit? You are so lucky. I would love to meet that guy," Kyle said, his eyes lighting up.

"I'm sure we can arrange that. He's pretty tight with Matt, so I'm in good with him. His fiancée, Lyric, is really sweet and seems to like me. She's the one who invited me to the house after the game."

"Oh, wow. What's his house like?"

"Huge. Like you would expect. I mean, I didn't get the grand tour or anything since we hung out in the basement, but even that was impressive. It looks just like a real bar you'd find in a restaurant. Dark woodgrain bar top with lots of stools, plus he's also got tables and chairs. They must love to entertain because you can pack a lot of people in there."

"Who else was there?" he asked, eyes wide with fascination.

"Matt of course. Angel Jimenez, Derek Jones, and Clay Williams."

"That is so cool," Kyle said.

Some people might think a person making head groundskeeper for a major league team was cool, too. But I guess Kyle was not one of those people.

I sighed deeply, hating how this conversation made me feel. Yesterday had been so much better. When I was excited and happy about my new job. I knew that feeling wouldn't go away just because of Kyle, but I hated how right now it felt like he was ruining my triumph.

"What's the matter with you?" Kyle asked, finally noticing my irritation.

"Sorry I'm not as exciting as Brady Keaton or those other guys."

"What are you talking about?"

"I just can't believe you didn't call or text or say *anything* yesterday, and today you seem bored out of your mind when I talk about my job. But when it comes to talking about famous baseball players, you're all about it," I said irritably.

"Well, I was busy," Kyle said defensively.

"You didn't even pitch yesterday."

"That doesn't mean I didn't have tons of stuff to do. Look, I'm sorry. Maybe you're right. I shoulda said something yesterday. I really am proud of you, Julia. You know that, right?"

No. I didn't know that.

"I guess."

"I am proud of you," he said, smiling at me and showing off those damned dimples. "I love you, Julia. I miss you."

My tight muscles relaxed, and I was already finding it hard to stay mad at him.

"I miss you, Kyle. I really do. Call me tonight and let me know how your pitching outing went."

"Okay. I will, baby."

Sighing, I touched the screen once more before hanging up.

10

___

JULIA

The Baltimore Bay Birds had just returned from a road trip, and a bunch of the guys planned to meet up at Brady's bar that evening. Once again, Lyric invited me to join. It was such an honor to hang out with all the players. I'd always been tight with Matt, and that probably helped the guys accept me right away. I rather doubted that most head groundkeepers got to hang out with the team, and I enjoyed every second of it.

Poor Kyle. I knew he would have given anything to be where I was right now. Sitting on a barstool with Matt to my left and Brady Keaton's fiancée to my right. Brady himself was serving us drinks, as usual. I truly had the best job in the world.

After downing two shots, I switched to beer. I think it impressed the guys that I could hold my liquor—the result of being a pretty hard partier in college.

"Hey, Angel," I said to him across the bar. "Lemme see the latest pictures. I know you got some new ones."

Grinning, he fished his phone out of his pocket. He abandoned his bar stool and came over to show me photos of his precious two-year-old son, Enrique, and his pretty wife, Jana. I hadn't met her yet, but Brady said she was great.

"Good-lookin' kid," I told him.

"All his mama, I assure you," Angel said, his warm brown eyes filled with affection for his family. "You thinkin' about having kids after you get hitched?"

"I would love to have kids. Just not right away," I said, and Angel nodded. "Got a lot going on now with the new job and all that. Plus, you know all about the minor league life. You can't really settle down anywhere permanent since you never know where you'll wind up playing."

"Yeah, I know how that is for sure," he said. "I was really lucky to be signed here in Baltimore. Jana's job is in Maryland and we're very fortunate to live together year-round."

"That is fortunate," I said, picturing Kyle's dimply smile and missing him deeply.

"Welp, I better head out and try to get some sleep. Enrique's not so much for sleeping in," Angel said, looking tired but happy.

"Have a good one," I said, hoisting my beer mug in the air to him.

I turned around to find our left fielder, Clay Williams, had wandered in while I'd been talking with Angel.

"Hey there, Clay," I said. "You looked great out there in New York yesterday."

Clay had blasted a three-run shot at last night's game, which had helped lead the Bay Birds to victory.

"Thank ye, thank ye," he said, tipping an imaginary hat to me.

Wordlessly, I squeezed Matt's shoulder. I knew he didn't want my pity, but I wanted to acknowledge his struggles. He was still having a rough time; he hadn't hit well on the road. He nodded grimly at me, which made my heart hurt.

My anger rose, remembering Kyle's glee at Matt's misfortune. I could never take pleasure in someone else's pain like that. I didn't know what the hell he was thinking sometimes.

Out of the corner of my eye, I saw Brady lock eyes with Lyric. Then very softly, he said, "Talk to her."

Lyric drew in a breath and nodded.

"So Julia," Lyric began. She seemed nervous. Whatever the reason, I wanted to put her mind at ease. She was a real sweetheart, and I could see us becoming good friends. We both had a lot of ambition, and she seemed like a very cool person that I wouldn't mind getting to know better.

"What's up?" I asked with an encouraging smile.

"I wanted to ask you something." She glanced over at Brady and then back at me.

"Fire away," I said. I drained the rest of my beer mug. In record time. Brady slid another one my way. Good thing I wasn't driving. Matt had offered me a lift.

"Well, it's kind of a favor I'm asking," Lyric said hesitantly.

"So hurry up and ask so I can point and laugh and say no," I said with a wink.

She laughed.

"For real, Lyric. It's cool. With all the free booze you and your man have given me, I figure I owe you one and then some."

"Okay. Well, as you know, Brady and I are getting married in July."

"During the All-Star break, right?"

"Yeah. And well, while Brady is Mr. Popularity and has a ton of guys he wants as groomsmen, I'm just one of those women who doesn't have a ton of girlfriends, you know?" Lyric sounded wistful as she spoke. "I've always been kind of a book nerd, and I'm always studying and overwhelmed all the time. It's not like I have much time for a social life."

I nodded. Medical school must be incredibly hard. I remembered Lyric telling me that she and Brady reconnected during their hectic schedules by cuddling together on the couch. On the outside, Brady was a huge, hulking athlete, but on the inside, he was a big teddy bear.

"So," she continued, "Brady has his brother, Eric, as his best man, and he wants Matt and Angel to be his groomsmen. And I, well, I don't have anybody for my side yet."

Lyric sounded ashamed of that fact, and it made me sad.

"I don't have any sisters or even female cousins, so ..."

"Lyric, are you asking me to be in your wedding?"

She winced and nodded.

"Are you kidding?" I exclaimed, probably way too loud, but that was me. "Try and stop me!"

Laughing, I engulfed her in a hug. She squeezed me back with great enthusiasm.

Once I let go, I said, "Oh my gosh, this is gonna be so much fun. I'm honored, Lyric. Truly."

"Thanks so much, Julia. I really appreciate it. I was afraid you were gonna think I was crazy for asking."

"Of course not. I understand completely where you're coming from. Although," I said sternly, "I make *no* guarantees about how I'm gonna look wearing a dress."

Matt chuckled. "Man, I'm looking forward to seeing that. Don't think I've *ever* seen you in a dress."

"You're gonna look just beautiful," Lyric said, relief shining in her eyes.

I felt bad that she'd clearly been stressing out over this conversation.

Turning to Brady behind the bar, I said, "Don't worry,

man. I'll take good care of your girl. I'll help her with wedding planning or anything she needs."

"That's great," he said with a grin. "Not only are you a bridesmaid, you're kinda like the maid of honor, I guess."

"Yeah, I guess you are," Lyric said apologetically.

"I love that!" I lifted my beer to toast Lyric. "This is gonna be so much fun. It's funny, you know. It occurs to me that I'm kinda in the same boat. I only have a brother, and a lot of my friends are guys. Lyric, I'd *love* to have you in my wedding in December. If you're available, I mean. I know your schedule is nuts."

Though I did have a few close girlfriends from Pennsylvania who were gonna be in my wedding, I left that part out for now. More than anything, I wanted Lyric to feel comfortable with her situation.

"No, the timing will be perfect actually. I should be on winter break by then. Julia, I would love to be a part of your wedding," Lyric said with a warm smile.

"Aren't you two girls the cutest things together?" Matt teased.

Wrapping an arm around him, I said, "You just make sure you reserve a dance for me at the wedding, Matt Jovey."

Matt glanced up at Brady and then back at me.

"Of course I will, Julia."

I grinned and squeezed him tighter.

11

———

MATT

Leaning on the railing of the dugout before the game, I glanced heavenward. Clouds were forming and the cool air smelled like rain. It felt rather like a metaphor for my life. Storm clouds gathering. I was a wreck having Julia around all the time, and it was messing up my hitting pretty badly. I wished it were possible to go on a long, cathartic run. That usually made me feel better and cleared my head.

I thought about all the runs I used to take in college. Breathing in the fresh country air with the lush mountains in the background. I'd felt so filled with hope for the future. Some of my dreams had come true, of course. Even mired in a terrible slump, I was still a Baltimore Bay Bird.

For now anyway.

My chest tightened just thinking about that. It would take more than a few bad games for the manager to bench me, but it certainly could happen.

"Looking kind of iffy for tonight," Brady observed, loudly chewing and popping his bubble gum.

"Sure does. Guess we'll have to see if we can squeeze in five innings before it lets loose."

I watched Julia, standing on the warning track and studying the iPad she used for weather tracking. Long curly hair secured in a ponytail under her Baltimore Bay Birds cap, she was the picture of sporty professionalism. Her presence here still pained me, but I genuinely enjoyed watching her in action.

Everyone here loved Julia. She'd become fast friends with administrative assistants, the cleaning crew, and most of the players on the team. Her predecessor was an older man by the name of Chuck Berrone. Nice guy and did a lovely job on the field, but he was all business and didn't socialize much. Julia was every bit as popular at the stadium as she had been in high school and in college. People felt good just being around her. As she'd mentioned at Brady's bar last night, many of her friends were male, but women tended to like her just as much as the guys. She was an incredibly attractive woman, but she wasn't snobby about it. Julia exuded a welcoming vibe that invited everyone toward her light.

Game time arrived, and so far the rain had held off. I'd started off the season batting cleanup, which meant I was fourth at bat. The strongest hitters were up first, and the cleanup position was designed to drive them home should one or more of the first three batters manage to get on base. That was before I started to utterly suck at hitting. Now, I batted seventh. As painful as it was to be demoted, I understood it was for the good of the team.

My fielding remained strong, however, with Brady and I still turning double plays well together. That would hopefully buy me a little time to get my act together before the manager took any drastic actions.

For my first plate appearance in the second inning, I struck out. Try as I might, I could no longer seem to judge the speed and position of the ball as it sailed toward me. It got to the point where I'd swung at so many pitches that were too high or too low that it made me afraid to swing at all. Which explained why I managed to strike out while barely swinging at the pitches.

Angry and humiliated, I vowed to swing like hell at my next at bat and quit being so goddamned intimidated out there. I was up again in the fourth inning. Clenching my jaw, I fought hard to focus. I swung at the first pitch. I could have sworn it was straight up the middle, but it turned out to be a ball and not a strike. I let the next two pitches pass by. One was a ball and one was a strike. Obviously, I was still not seeing the ball well. I connected with the next pitch, but weakly. The infielder caught the ball easily.

A fabulous way to end the inning *and* a rally, since I had left two guys stranded on base.

Grimly, I returned to the dugout where no one dared speak to me. It was an unwritten rule—and a good one— that you did not bother a man who was struggling mightily at bat. Nothing could be said to make the guy feel better, and every single player on the team knew what a slump felt like because we'd all been there.

Then it started to rain. Just a few drops at first, but Julia had undoubtedly watched the weather closely and knew more than the rest of us what to expect. Within seconds, she had dispatched her team to start rolling out the tarp. The huge metal roll was heavy, and it was much harder to move than most people knew. In a very public and embarrassing debacle a few years ago, a disorganized ground crew struggled for more than twenty minutes to roll out the tarp and get it straight on the field, much to the delight of the sportscasters covering the event. It wasn't our team, thank good-ness, but no doubt that kind of nightmare haunted the dreams of people in Julia's profession. Groundskeeping was one of those things nobody really noticed until something went wrong.

I found myself smiling as I watched Julia's team cover the field with expert precision. Rain delays could be very stressful in her line of work, but they also gave her a chance to shine.

My career might be in the toilet right now, but it filled me with sheer elation to see how happy Julia was as she excelled in her dream job.

That's my girl.

Yeah. If *only*.

12

JULIA

Kyle was on his way to my place for a visit, and I could not have been more excited. It had been over a month since we'd seen each other. The Baltimore Bay Birds were off on a road trip, and Kyle's team was playing in Virginia, so he had time to see me since he wasn't scheduled to pitch again until the team returned to South Carolina.

I'd cleaned up my tiny apartment as best I could before he got here. I'd wrapped up all my field maintenance at the ballpark early this morning, so I was free and clear until Kyle had to leave tomorrow. My plan was to make love all afternoon and then maybe go to dinner. We could always order in if we weren't ready to leave the bedroom yet. Lack of sex was a serious drawback to a long-distance relation-ship. Being surrounded by hunky, muscular baseball players all the time wasn't easy when you had to remain celibate half the year. I missed being touched so much, and frankly, I could use a good hard pounding right now. And I knew Kyle could give me what I needed. He always did.

At long last, I heard a knock at the door. It was so weird

for my fiancé to knock like some stranger, but there was no sense in bothering to get a key for him. He rarely came to Baltimore during the season.

Rushing to the door, I flung it open. My heart soared when I saw him, and I pulled him in close for an embrace before letting him say a word.

"I've missed you so much," I said.

"Missed you too," Kyle said, squeezing me back lightly.

"Come in, come in," I said, ushering him in the door. "My apartment makes our place in PA look like the Taj Mahal, doesn't it?"

He chuckled. "Yeah, it kinda does. Don't feel bad. My place in South Carolina is much worse. I'm not even kidding."

"That's too bad," I said. I hated thinking of him being stuck in some crappy apartment. Things would get better, though. I was making a lot more money now, and soon we would be able to afford nicer things. But now wasn't the time to bring that up. Kyle could be sensitive about that kind of thing. He wanted to be the breadwinner and someday, when he made it to the majors, he would be.

"Where's your suitcase?" I asked.

"Umm, it's in the car," Kyle said, running his hands through his hair.

"You looked tired. Are you okay?"

"Yeah." He hesitated. "Well, not really."

His expression made me worry that something was wrong.

Oh my God, don't tell me he got cut from the team.

Maybe he'd lied about the break in his schedule and he was here because the team had let him go. Or maybe he'd been traded to a team even farther away.

It was silly to let my imagination run wild. Best to figure

out right away what was going on.

"Come on and sit down."

I led him over to the couch and took his hand in mine. "Whatever's going on with you, it's gonna be okay. We'll get through it together."

Kyle groaned. "You're not making this easy."

"What?" I asked. I thought I was being supportive.

"I don't think this ... we ...*us* ... as a couple ... is really working out anymore," he said, wincing as he avoided my gaze.

It took me several seconds to register the words that had just come out of his mouth.

"Wait ... What?"

Shaking, I let go of his hand.

"This can't be a total surprise to you, Julia," he said, finally looking at me. "We haven't been, you know, exactly connecting much lately."

"Of course we're not connecting. We live in different states," I exclaimed, my panic level rising by the second.

"But it's more than that. It just feels like we don't really have that spark anymore."

"What are you talking about? Where is all this coming from?"

"I don't know, Julia," Kyle said, sounding impatient and irritable. "It just feels like things have fizzled out between us. I don't even know if it's something I can explain."

Kyle doesn't want me anymore. He doesn't love me.

I was far too stunned to cry or even to speak. A heavy, physical pain shot through my chest as if he had punched me in the heart. I felt dizzy, disoriented, and bewildered.

This cannot be happening.

"Are you ... are you ... breaking off our engagement?"

"I'm really sorry, Julia."

We sat there on the couch not speaking a word for so long that I lost track of time. Eventually, I staggered to my feet and walked over to the window in my tiny living room and stared outside where the rest of the world kept going as if my entire life hadn't been completely upended. I watched cars drive up and down the busy streets of Baltimore. People strolled down the road with takeout containers or walked their dogs. I saw a family carefully waiting their turn at a crosswalk.

As the shock began to wear off, panic set in. My mind raced and my heart thumped hard in my chest. Surely there must be some kind of solution to whatever relationship problems we were having. Drawing in a deep breath, I started to think more clearly.

I walked slowly back over to the couch and sat down next to Kyle.

"I'm sorry that you feel like we're not connecting anymore," I said, my voice quavering. "But this all seems so sudden. I think we just need to slow down for a bit. All relationships take work. It's amazing that we've managed to make this long-distance thing work for as long as we have."

"That's true," he said, giving me some hope that we could still salvage our relationship.

My nerves continued to settle and logic began to take over.

"This reminds me of what I've heard about military marriages. Everybody loves those videos online where a soldier comes home to surprise his family. I know I do. But I've read that it can be hard when a spouse comes home after a long absence. Military wives and husbands say it can be like having a stranger in the house, and they have to get to know each other all over again. Maybe that's what we need to do."

"I understand what you're saying," Kyle said cautiously. "But I don't think that's gonna work with us."

My breath caught in my throat. Panic rose up in me all over again.

I was losing him.

"Kyle, you can't just give up on us! Not after all this time. We've been together for so long, and now you just want to throw it all away?"

"It's not like I want to, Julia," he said, his face twisting into a painful grimace. "You have no idea how much I hate hurting you. But being together ... It's just not the right thing for me anymore."

His words stabbed my heart.

"We should at least try counseling before we throw in the towel, Kyle."

"That wouldn't do any good."

"You don't know that! How do you know if we haven't even—"

"I met someone else, Julia," Kyle snapped.

A fresh wave of shock washed over me as I registered his words, delivered far more harshly than I deserved.

Kyle sighed deeply. "I didn't want to tell you that. I didn't want to get into it and make you feel worse, but you're not giving me much choice here."

"Who is she?" I demanded, both wanting and not wanting to know.

"Just some friend of one of the other player's wives," he said with a dismissive wave.

"What's her name? What does she do for a living?"

"What does it matter?" Kyle responded with the gall to sound irritated with my questions.

"Don't I have a right to know who is responsible for destroying my entire future?"

"It's not her fault." He spoke with tenderness in his voice about this other woman. Of everything he had done to me today, somehow that hurt worst of all. I could not remember a time when he talked about me with that kind of affection.

"Answer my questions. You owe me at least that."

"Daria Miller. She's a real estate agent."

Already, I was sorry I'd asked. Having a name to go with this nightmare somehow made it much worse. Would her name someday be Daria Nolan?

I no longer had a fiancé. I was struck by the realization that I might never have children. If I did, it wouldn't be with Kyle. There would be no wedding, no honeymoon. No future. No happily ever after.

The shock of it all was too much for me to handle.

I raced to the bathroom and vomited violently.

After rinsing my mouth with mouthwash, I splashed water on my face. I caught a glimpse of myself in the mirror and was frightened by what I saw—my face splotchy and red. My expression held a look of terror and grief.

Though I knew I would regret it, I knew what I had to do. I had to get this next part over with.

I pulled my cell phone out of my back pocket and looked up Daria Miller, real estate, South Carolina. And there she was.

She was beautiful.

Long dark brown hair, pretty blue eyes. Her nails looked freshly painted, her fingers and wrists adorned with fancy jewelry. Beautiful, incredibly feminine.

All the things I wasn't.

Maybe Kyle couldn't love a tomboy like me after all.

The pain was so excruciating that I could hardly breathe.

I walked back to the living room. Kyle stood up. He

gasped when he saw me and put a hand over his heart. He took a step toward me, but I held up my hand to stop him.

"Get out of here. *Now*."

"Look, it wasn't like I cheated or anything," he said. "I was waiting for ... you know ... until ..."

"You were waiting to screw her until you could get rid of me," I said.

Kyle said nothing, which was all the answer I needed.

"I said get *out*."

He sighed with exasperation, as if I were the only unreasonable one.

I watched him walk out, and he never looked back. I stared at the closed door for a long time before sinking back down on the couch.

For the first time in my life, I felt utterly lost and alone. I was usually so ambitious, raring to go and ready for anything. Now, I had no idea what to do. Where to go. How to cope with life after Kyle.

I spent the rest of the afternoon and evening in a daze. Knowing there was no way in hell I could sleep, I headed to the ballpark after dark.

Old Bay Stadium was deserted, which was what I needed right now. I had full access to pretty much everywhere in the ballpark since I frequently arrived very early in the morning and sometimes stayed late at night. My presence wouldn't arouse any suspicion, even if anyone had been here.

I walked around the warning track several times to help get rid of my nervous energy. It was quite dark with no stadium lights on, but the lights of downtown Baltimore were bright enough that I could see where I was going. I tired myself out a bit, then sat down on top of the dugout.

Closing my eyes, I took in a deep, calming breath and let

it out. I counted my blessings. I still had the best job in the whole world. I knew I would have the love and support of my brother and the rest of the family. I had Matt and my newer friends on the team. As horrible and painful as a broken engagement was, I supposed it was better than having to endure a divorce. Or worse, being left at the altar. My God, that would have been humiliating.

As if this wasn't bad enough.

I opened my eyes, already having a hard time looking on the bright side. I'd been dumped by my fiancé. He'd grown bored of me. I loved Kyle Nolan, but I wasn't enough for him. I wasn't pretty enough, I guess. I'd never known him to be the type to fall for a girly-girl, but I must not have known him as well as I'd thought.

I sat there for a while, hoping that the peaceful space of the ballpark would steady my nerves. It helped a little, but the still of the night could not protect me from the horrible light of day.

Tomorrow, I would have to begin the process of telling everyone that my life had been blown apart in a matter of minutes. One thing I knew for sure, I was not about to tell anyone that Kyle had been the one to end it. No one had to know he left me for another woman. I would just tell people it was mutual and leave it at that.

I felt so incredibly stupid. Just a few hours ago, I had expected Kyle to be happy to see me. I'd thought he would hold me and kiss me and make love to me for hours. Instead, he'd utterly rejected me. Thrown me away like a piece of unwanted garbage. Which was exactly what I felt like.

I got to my feet and trudged toward my tiny, empty apartment.

As exhausted as I was, I doubted sleep would come.

13

MATT

I got a text from Julia asking me to come to her office as soon as I got to the stadium. When I asked her if everything was okay, she texted *Not really.*

Gym bag in hand, I jumped into the car and rushed to Old Bay Stadium, white-knuckling the steering wheel the whole way. Her performance as head groundskeeper was impeccable, so surely that couldn't be a problem, right? God, I hoped not. She loved her job, and she was so happy.

What if something had happened to Jerry?

Julia would never break tragic news to me over the phone. It made sense that if my best friend had been killed in a car wreck, she would tell me in person.

Having worked myself into full-blown panic mode by the time I reached Julia's office, I rapped hard on her office door.

"Come in," Julia said softly.

I hurried inside, shut the door behind me, and sat down across from her.

"Are you all right?" I asked, eyes wide.

"Oh, Matt," she said, her hazel eyes full of sorrow. "I'm

sorry. I didn't mean to freak you out by sending you such a vague text. Yeah, I'm okay. Nobody died or anything."

I let out a deep breath, only partially relieved. It wasn't the worst-case scenario, thank God, but it must still be bad.

Julia slumped in her seat across from me, her eyes still filled with sadness. "Kyle … well, Kyle and me … We broke off the engagement."

I stared at her. Of all the things I'd expected her to say, that never once crossed my mind for a second.

"You what?"

"It's over," she said, her voice quaking.

"Julia, I'm so sorry," I said, and I truly was. Later on, I would probably feel utterly relieved; happy, even. But that wasn't possible now. Not while Julia was in so much pain. "I just … I can't believe it. This is so sudden. Isn't it?"

She'd never said a word about any problems between the two of them. Selfishly, I could admit I would have welcomed news of discord between them. But there'd never been anything more than the usual disagreements as far as I knew.

"Not as sudden as you might think. There were signs, I guess," Julia said wearily. "We weren't really connecting anymore. Somehow, we'd always managed to make the long-distance thing work, but I think it finally got to be too much."

I wracked my brain, desperately trying to think of something—anything—to say to make her feel better. Guilt tore through me; I'd dreamed of this moment. Of course in my own ludicrous fantasies, Julia broke it off with Kyle because she realized she was in love with me.

"It was mutual. We both decided it's what's best, but …"

Her lovely eyes filled with tears, and I could hardly bear it. I might not be the hugging type, but she sure as hell was.

Besides, I was overwhelmed with the need to hold her close.

I got up and walked over to where she sat behind the desk. I held out my hands. Smiling sadly, she allowed me to pull her to her feet. I wrapped my arms around her, pulling her into an embrace. How I ached to protect her from this agony. More than anything, I wished I could take the pain away from her and bear it myself.

Tenderly stroking her hair, I closed my eyes and breathed her in. She still smelled of the outdoors, of adventures in the grass and the dirt. I loved her so much, and I hated to think of her experiencing even a fraction of the lovesick torture I'd endured for so many years.

"I wish I knew what to say, what to do, to make you feel better."

Sniffling a little, she drew in a shuddery breath. "Thank you, Matt. It helps so much to have you here with me."

Julia let go of me, and my body instantly felt cold without her in my arms.

"Listen," she said, her voice still shaky. "I could really use your help with something."

"Of course. Name it. *Anything.*"

"If you could kind of let people know what's going on. I'll tell my own crew, of course. But if you could tell the team and whoever else you think needs to know. I mean, people ask me about wedding plans all the time, and I just can't—"

Julia swallowed hard, fighting not to cry.

"Of course. I understand. I don't want you to have to talk about this anymore than necessary. I got you covered."

"I knew you would," she said.

She threw her arms around me and kissed my cheek. "Love you so much, Matt."

"I love you too, Julia."

Julia blinked at me. "Wow. That's the first time I've ever heard you say that back to me, dude."

My face heated a little. I knew she noticed, too, because she smiled.

"Yeah well, I guess I was just saving it for when you really needed to hear it."

"I sure did need that today." Tenderly caressing my face, she said, "Thanks, Matt. You're the best friend any girl could ever ask for."

I stifled a groan, but it was probably best that she reminded me we were still just friends. Breaking up with her fiancé didn't mean she would suddenly go for me after all these years. I would do well to remember that.

After she let go of me, I asked, "Is there anything else I can do?"

"Not that I can think of," she said.

I closed her door on my way out, to give her some privacy. I dreaded breaking this awful news to my teammates, but I knew it had to be done. Usually the type to keep my head down, I avoided gossip and discussing people's personal business. Still, I understood that this situation was different. Julia wanted me to help spread the word, and it would save her a lot of heartache in having to deal with well-meaning people who might innocently ask painful questions.

I waited until several guys had showed up to the clubhouse before I cleared my throat to make the announcement.

"Hey. Listen up, guys. I need to talk to you for a second."

Everyone froze when I spoke. It was weird, but it made sense. I wasn't in the habit of saying much unless it was important, so people knew something was up.

"I've got some bad news. Julia wanted me to let people know that she and her fiancé split up."

"Are you serious?" Brady practically shouted. Everybody knew she and I were close friends from way back, but Brady was the only one who knew my true feelings and how her breakup affected me.

"Yeah," I said, shooting him a warning look to be cool. He would never blab my secret on purpose, but he didn't always think before he spoke. Brady nodded, catching my drift.

"Aw man," Angel said sadly. "That's too bad. I'm real sorry to hear that."

Looking somber, Brady asked, "Is she okay?"

"She's doing all right, I guess. It was a mutual decision. Probably for the best and all of that, but it's still tough. I just wanted to help spread the word so people won't keep asking her questions about the wedding and everything."

Many of the guys nodded, and all of them looked somber. Everybody loved Julia around here, and I felt better seeing how the guys really cared about her. She was always the one lifting everybody else up with a smile and encouraging words when they needed a friend. I knew she would get the same kind of treatment now that she needed a boost.

"Feel free to discreetly let members of the staff know as you feel appropriate. You know how Julia is," I said, unable to suppress a smile as I spoke about her. "She's friends with just about everybody."

Nods and smiles from all around. Yeah. They knew.

"Thanks. I really appreciate your help on this. And I know she does, too."

Shaking his head, Clay said, "That really sucks. Give her my best, you know? I don't want to just go up to her and start talkin' about it or anything. So just, you know, tell her I'm sorry and all."

Several of the guys murmured their agreement with Clay's statement.

"I will man. I'll tell her you guys are thinking about her."

With that, they started to disperse as they headed out for batting practice.

Brady eyed me curiously. "You doing okay?"

"Yeah. It's like … I'm not even sure what to think. Sure as hell can't be happy about it. Not when she's in so much pain."

"I get that. Listen, if there's anything me or Lyric can do for her, you be sure and let us know."

"Thanks, man. I appreciate it."

Brady clapped me on the back and then headed out to the field.

Sinking down on the bench, I indulged in a moment or two of quiet before joining the team out on the field.

14

JULIA

I'd arranged to meet with Lyric for lunch to discuss her wedding plans. Naturally, that was before Kyle had broken off our engagement. She texted me as soon as she heard the news, graciously telling me it was perfectly fine to call off our lunch date. I figured I could use a friend right now, so I insisted I wanted to meet up with her as planned.

When I arrived at Robby's Deli, located not far from the stadium, Lyric greeted me with the same sympathetic smile I'd been getting from people all week. They meant well, but I really didn't want their pity.

Still, I understood where they were coming from. Had it been anyone else, I wouldn't have known what to say either. I did my best to cheer other people up when they were down, but it was hard to know exactly what to do or say sometimes.

"It's good to see you," Lyric said uncertainly.

"You too. It's nice to be out with a girlfriend right now, you know?"

She smiled, seeming a little more at ease.

"You know how guys are." I punched her lightly on the shoulder and said in a gruff voice, "How's it goin', girl?"

Lyric laughed. "Yeah, I know what you mean." Glancing at the menu up on the wall, she asked. "Do you know what you want?"

"No, but I'm sure I'll figure it out once we get through the line."

We joined the queue, ordered, and brought our food back to our table. Despite having skipped breakfast, I wasn't hungry. Still, I knew I needed to keep my energy up, so I'd force myself to eat.

"How are you doing?" Lyric asked, eying me carefully. I didn't envy her, being stuck here with me. What do you say to somebody whose wedding was just called off?

"I'm not sure," I answered uncertainly as I picked at my turkey and cheese sandwich.

"I can understand that," she said gently.

I still didn't know Lyric all that well, but there was something about her that put me at ease every time I spoke with her. Like I could talk to her about anything. Even so, I still couldn't bring myself to tell her or anyone else the truth about what had happened between me and Kyle.

Lyric ate her sandwich quietly for a moment, probably waiting for me to elaborate on my situation. As much as I wanted to vent my feelings to her, I wasn't sure how to get started.

"Julia," she began. "I want you to know that you can talk to me about it if you want. If you feel comfortable, that is. But I also understand if you'd rather not."

I nodded gratefully. Her words were exactly what I needed to hear. And it wasn't just her words that made me feel better. Lyric's warm and soothing demeanor told me I could trust her. She wouldn't judge me, and she wouldn't divulge anything I told her to anybody. She would simply listen.

"I've been saying to everybody that it had been coming for a long time. That things hadn't been working for a while, but that's not really true," I began cautiously. "The truth is that our breakup was rather sudden."

Lyric met my gaze and nodded with sympathy. It helped to admit that much about the breakup. I'd been utterly blindsided by Kyle's rejection, and I felt totally lost. Though I still couldn't confide the whole ugly truth, part of me wished I could talk to Lyric about the terrifying reality of having someone suddenly fall out of love with you. How it made you question everything.

"I've been with him so long that it's like I can't even imagine a future without him," I said, my voice quaking and tears threatening to spill.

"That must be incredibly difficult," she said. "It's impossible to imagine my life without Brady, and I haven't been with him as long as you and Kyle were together. You met in college, right?"

"Yeah."

"That's hard, Julia. I'm so sorry."

I deeply appreciated her sympathy, but the breakup filled me with shame. Thank God I hadn't told anyone that it had been all Kyle's idea. To have the whole world know that a man had proposed to me and then changed his mind was more than I could handle. I had no idea what Kyle was telling other people, but at least he lived far away and we didn't travel in any of the same circles.

I was suddenly struck with paranoia that people would find out. That my crew and all the team members would discover that my fiancé had dumped me. I'd worked so damned hard my whole life to get where I was now. To earn the respect of people in the sports business. I couldn't ever let anyone know the truth.

"It's all for the best, really," I said, putting on the brave face I'd been faking ever since Kyle cut me loose with zero warning.

"It's sad when things like that happen," Lyric said. "As painful as this all must be, I guess it's better to find out before you get married."

"That's for sure. A broken engagement is hard enough. A divorce would be complicated. But we should move on to happier things," I said. "How are the wedding plans going?"

Lyric looked a bit uncomfortable and, once again, I felt bad about the situation I'd put her in. Who the hell wanted a sad sack, jilted bridesmaid in her wedding? I was determined not to let my misfortune mess up her special day. She still needed me to be in her wedding, and I had no intention of letting her down.

"Julia, about that. You don't have to—"

"Lyric, I still want to be in your wedding. I don't want you worrying for a second about that."

"But I *am* worried. This all must be very hard on you. You seem to be handling everything really well and all. I just know if it were me, I wouldn't even want to attend a wedding, let alone be in one."

"It's fine. Really."

"Look, you don't have to decide right now."

"Lyric. I have decided. I'm *in*."

She sighed softly. "I'm still not sure if it's a good idea."

That now-familiar wave of humiliation washed over me again. It felt like Lyric was rejecting me too. It was all too much to bear.

"Unless you don't want me to be in your wedding. I'll understand if—"

"Of *course* I want you in my wedding. I just can't stand the idea of causing you any more pain, Julia," she said, her sweet blue eyes filled with sadness.

The tension in my body eased, and I realized I was just being paranoid. Lyric had such a good heart.

"I feel like this is something I have to do," I said, not realizing it was true until the words came out of my mouth. "Like I have to show up and be in the wedding and prove to everybody that I'm not some sad, pathetic, broken woman. Everybody's feeling so damn sorry for me right now, and I hate it."

Nodding, Lyric said, "I get that. I really do."

"Good," I said firmly.

"Still, I want you to know ... it's okay if you change your mind. I'll understand."

"Thanks. I appreciate that."

"You're a strong woman," she told me with a smile.

I shrugged like it was no big deal.

"It's not always gonna be this hard," Lyric said softly. Her compassion made me wonder if I should just open up and tell her everything. But I didn't. I just couldn't. "Over time, it will get better. I promise."

"Thank you," I said quietly. Something in the way she spoke made me believe her. She was right. My heart hurt like hell, but the pain wouldn't be this severe forever.

The queasiness in my stomach began to abate, and I was actually hungry enough to eat my sandwich.

It felt like a small but important step toward recovery.

15

———

MATT

The shock of Julia's breakup with Kyle was starting to wear off, and I was relieved that I wouldn't have to endure a wedding ceremony where she pledged her heart to another man. She was suffering tremendously, though, and I chastised myself for any measure of happiness I felt with her fiancé being out of the picture. Deep down, I'd hoped that Julia might someday break up with him, but I'd totally abandoned that notion once they got engaged. I hadn't dreamed they'd break off their engagement.

And I was sure Julia had never planned on that, either.

Julia had spent the last week busying herself with work. She hadn't been her usual effervescent self of course, but she still wore a smile and was friendly with everyone. The pain in her eyes haunted me, though. I couldn't imagine how much energy it took for her to keep that brave face on all the time.

More than anything, I wanted a chance to be alone with her. I had no intention of making a move on her. Not only had she fiercely friend-zoned me, only a monster would hit on a woman who'd just had her heart broken. The breakup might have been mutual, but Julia was still hurting badly. All I wanted was some time with my friend, away from crowds and coworkers, where she could be real with me and talk if she felt up to it.

That was why I showed up at Old Bay Stadium at 5am on a Tuesday, a full twelve hours before batting practice. Ever the workhorse, Julia arrived long before anybody else on her crew. And I knew how much she loved quiet mornings alone at the ballpark.

"What in the world are you doing here at this ungodly hour?" Julia asked as she walked toward me on the warning track near the dugout.

"I wanted to see you."

"I see you every day, Matt." She looked understandably confused.

"I wanted to catch you alone. See if you were okay."

"You're so sweet," Julia said with a smile. She threw her arms around me, hugging me tight. After letting go, she wrapped her arm around me and led me to the dugout. There, she expertly climbed the metal railing that led to the seats closest to the field and walked on top of the dugout. It made me chuckle the way she scaled obstacles like a kid climbing a tree.

She sat down on top of the dugout with her legs swinging over the edge. Patting the spot next to her, she said, "Well, come on. What are you waiting for?"

I climbed the railing much less gracefully than she had. I was muscular and athletic, but I was also really tall, which made it a bit harder.

I took a seat next to her. She squeezed my shoulder tight and let go. Times like this I wished I could just pull her into my arms and hold her close like a lover instead of settling for the short hugs of a good friend.

We sat in silence for a few moments, gazing out at the dark, empty field.

"This is nice," she said, and I nodded. "I love being here at this time of the day. Soothes my nerves."

"How are you doing with everything?" I asked.

Julia sighed deeply. "Still processing it all, I guess. It all feels so strange. He was always just *there*, you know?"

Yeah. I know.

"It feels like a death." She spoke softly, sadly. So different from her usual tone. My heart ached for her. "Everything happened so fast. It really feels like Kyle died very suddenly. And it's like I have to remind myself a hundred times a day that he's gone. We were together so many years, and he was such a huge part of my life. Even living apart like we did. So many times I catch myself thinking *I have to call Kyle tonight,* or when something funny or interesting happens on the job, I think *I can't wait to tell Kyle.*"

Julia's sweet face crumpled and her voice shook. "And then I remember. I can't call him. He's not in my life anymore. Just like that. He's just ... *gone.*"

I wrapped my arm around her, and she rested her head on my shoulder. I suddenly longed for my old familiar pain over her, because it was better than watching her suffer. It felt as if my agony had transferred to Julia, and it was horrific.

"I promise, it's not always gonna hurt this bad," I told her.

Lifting her head to look at me, she said, "That's what Lyric said. And I'd like to believe her, but your situation kinda freaks me out."

"My situation? What are you talking about?"

"That girl who broke your heart in college," Julia said, her expression slightly panicked. "After all this time, you never got over her, Matt. Whoever she was, you loved her so much that you were never able to let her go. You told me yourself. Every woman you try to date, you're mentally comparing her to the one that got away."

I didn't know what to say to that. I wanted to tell her that she would get over Kyle. That her situation was totally different. But what if it wasn't?

"What was her name anyway? I don't think you ever told me."

"I don't want to talk about it," I said, my body tensing up. My reaction to her question clearly panicked her more, and I knew I had to say *something* to make her feel better. "Trust me, it's not the same thing. It just isn't."

Julia shook her head, her expression more despondent than ever before.

"Would it help if I told you that I never really liked Kyle?"

"You didn't?" she gasped.

I'd always disliked the guy, mostly because she was with him instead of me. Still, there were other things I wasn't crazy about when it came to him.

"Not really. It's not like I knew him all that well. At first, I thought he was perfect for you."

Kyle had seemed an ideal match for Julia when they first met. He was funny, charming, and outgoing, just like her. Not a broody, quiet, boring guy like me.

"Then later, I'm not sure exactly what it was about him I didn't like. I guess I just had a nagging feeling you could do better."

Julia considered my words.

"You must have felt the same way if you broke up with him."

"I guess," she said sadly.

I hated seeing her so upset, so I wracked my brain to come up with more reasons why she was better off without Kyle.

"You know when you're hanging out in Brady's basement and laughing and joking around with all the guys? I always like seeing you like that. You're always the life of the party. But Kyle usually looked annoyed when you got loud out in public, and I guess that always kind of bothered me. I don't know. It felt like he was trying to stifle you, suppress your personality or something. It wasn't right."

"Huh," she said thoughtfully.

Though I'd just been trying to cheer her up, it occurred to me how true my words were. I'd never realized how much that had annoyed me about Kyle until now. Who the hell was he to try to crush her spirit?

"I guess I just need to be on my own for a while," she said. "I have to relearn how to be single. It's been so long."

"Yeah, it certainly has."

The years had seemed long to me, to be sure. I'd never gotten used to seeing Julia with Kyle. It hurt to see them together right up to the end.

"I'm supposed to be in Brady's wedding, you know."

I winced, having forgotten about that.

"Are you sure you're up for it?"

"Yeah, I think it will be okay. Lyric is turning out to be a good friend, and I want to be there for her. Besides, I was never the type who dreamed about my own wedding since I was a little girl. It was weird how even when I was engaged, I kinda dragged my feet on planning the wedding."

"Maybe subconsciously you knew you didn't really want to get married."

Julia shook her head. "No, that really wasn't it. It was just like I thought more about being married than the actual ceremony. That's the way it should be. Nothing wrong with having the wedding of your dreams if that's your thing, but people definitely get too caught up in that and forget what it's really about. Marriage. Spending your life with someone."

She faltered as she spoke, and I could see the raw pain in her eyes.

"I really did want to marry Kyle. And honestly, I'm not sure what went wrong."

At a loss for words, I slid my arm around her. She rested her head on my shoulder.

"I'm glad you're here, Matt."

"I'm always here for you, Julia. Always."

We sat together in silence on the dugout, watching the sun rise over the ballfield.

16

JULIA

My hands flew to my mouth as I gasped out loud. Slowly lowering my hands, I whispered, "That's it."

"Right?" Lyric exclaimed, her eyes wide.

I stared at her as she modeled what could only be described as the perfect wedding dress for her. Lyric's mother had told her she would know when she found the right gown, but neither one of us had really believed it after having searched through hundreds of dresses. Her mother had come with us on the first two dress shopping trips, but today it was just the two of us.

I didn't know what it was about this dress, but Lyric was positively radiant in it. Funny how we both knew immediately it was the right choice. Stepping back to admire her beauty, I smiled as she happily spun around in front of the mirror. With her pale skin, dark hair, and bright blue eyes, she looked like a Disney princess in the lovely beaded and sparkly gown that flared out slightly at the bottom without being too poofy.

Given my own situation, seeing a bride-to-be prepare for

her wedding should have been terribly painful, but for the most part it wasn't. Lyric was a dear friend to me now, and I enjoyed seeing her so happy. And Brady was such a good guy. The two of them were so much in love that I couldn't help but rejoice just being around them. Helping Lyric prepare for the wedding and having the privilege of being her maid of honor meant the world to me.

"Thanks so much for being here with me, Julia. I never would have found this dress if it weren't for you. I'd have settled a long time ago."

"Who would have thought me of all people would be the one to help with a dress?" I asked with a laugh. Lyric's wedding would be the first time in years I'd worn a dress. "I'm just so glad you found what you were looking for."

All this talking of not settling and finding what you're looking for had taken on a deeper meaning since Kyle and I broke up.

Still, I was grateful to be here with Lyric. This was one of those moments in life when you needed a girlfriend by your side, and I was happy to oblige. It wasn't always easy, though. There had been times over the last few weeks when I'd felt depressed and lonely. Lots of ups and downs, but today was a good day. It made me feel like I could handle being in the wedding.

THE DAY of the wedding was busy, which was good. As Lyric's maid of honor, I ran around like crazy making sure she had everything she needed to get ready for the early-evening ceremony. Brady had his brother, Eric, as his best man, and Angel and Matt as his groomsmen. In addition to me, Lyric had Angel's wife, Jana, and her Aunt Clara for her bridesmaids.

Like I'd told Matt, I hadn't spent much time fantasizing about my own wedding, so it didn't bother me all that much that I might always be a bridesmaid and never the bride, as the saying went. Besides, I was still pretty young. I could still meet somebody great and get married. Trouble was, I'd been burned so badly by Kyle that the thought of being with someone else terrified me.

Kyle had stopped loving me with no warning. He had fallen for somebody else when he was supposed to be with me. And it could happen again.

The hardest part was that I'd truly believed he loved me for who I was. The fact that he'd dumped me for a woman who was my opposite was frightening. Daria seemed so glamorous, so alluring. Apart from that, I kept thinking about Matt's comment that Kyle seemed annoyed by my personality. I'd always been the tomboyish type and yes, I could get loud sometimes. I was proud of who I was, and I wasn't about to change, especially not for a guy. Still, I found myself wondering if there was a man out there who could love me for who I really was. If not, I guess I would stay single.

Staring at myself in the mirror, I drew in a deep breath to gain control of my emotions. Today would be tough, but I would get through it for Lyric's sake.

It felt so strange to see myself in a dress. I had to admit, I didn't look half bad. Lyric had selected an off-the-shoulder, burgundy chiffon gown for the bridesmaids. Very classy, not to mention expensive, but Brady had footed the bill for everything. Normally, the bridesmaids would pay for their own dresses and shoes and all that, but considering the groom was a multi-millionaire, I didn't feel too bad about his contribution. He'd paid to get our hair and makeup done professionally and had even bought us matching purses to go with our dresses. It was all so decadent. As much fun as it was to indulge in all this fancy stuff, it wasn't my sort of thing. That made me even more grateful that I hadn't had to shell out a lot of money for a dress, shoes, and purse that I would likely never use again. Of course, I was more than happy to do whatever Lyric and Brady wanted for their special day. Serving as maid of honor had started out as a favor for a woman I hardly knew, but now Lyric and I were close friends. I couldn't imagine not being a part of her wedding now.

A half hour later while standing in the back of the church, I asked the beautiful bride, "You doing okay?" We were minutes away from walking down the aisle for the ceremony.

"Yeah. I think so," Lyric said, looking nervous as hell. She'd told me she had no qualms whatsoever about marrying Brady, but his celebrity status meant the wedding would garner a ton of attention. However, he was aware of Lyric's feelings and had promised not to let his fame get in the way of what was important.

"Remember what Brady told you," I said firmly to Lyric, and she nodded. He'd advised her to lock eyes with him as she walked down the aisle. That way, instead of stressing out about how many eyes were on her, she could focus on him.

"Right," she said. Then she drew in a deep breath to steady herself. She let it out slowly and turned to me. "Are *you* doing okay?"

Her pretty blue eyes were filled with concern, which was the last thing I wanted right now. This should be the happiest day of her life, and I didn't want her to waste one second of it worrying about me.

"I'm doing great," I said, smiling and lying through my teeth.

While I was genuinely happy for my friend, this day was already shaping up to be harder than I'd expected. All the preparation for the ceremony had kept me busy, but now that it was really happening, it would be incredibly tough to get through the wedding and the hours-long reception. A marathon celebration of love, filled with romantic songs and promises of happily ever after. Nobody deserved happiness more than Brady and Lyric, but I couldn't stop the deep, raw pain spreading through my chest as I stood there. Brady loved her so dearly. And Kyle had thrown me away like a piece of trash. Maybe that was too harsh, but that was how it felt.

"You look so beautiful, Lyric," I said, trying to steer her away from her concern for me. There would be plenty of time to talk with her about my hurt feelings after the honeymoon. Until then, I wanted the focus to be on her.

"Thanks," she said gratefully.

Her Aunt Clara gazed at her, admiring her gown. "You couldn't have chosen a more perfect wedding dress. You're gorgeous." Her eyes filling with tears, she reached over to embrace Lyric, careful not to smudge her makeup. "I'm so happy for you."

The processional song started up and Lyric gasped.

"You're gonna be just fine," Jana soothed. I'd gotten to know her pretty well during the wedding planning, and she was a real sweetheart. Still, she and her husband, Angel, were another perfect couple that made me feel worse about my current situation. God, I hated that about myself. I hated feeling bitter about other people's happiness. Angel and Jana loved each other dearly, and they were parents to an adorable little boy. I should be celebrating that, not feeling sorry for myself.

Jana began her procession down the aisle, and then Aunt Clara did the same. Then came my turn. Putting on my best smile, I began my trek down the aisle. I was sure to tread carefully. I hadn't worn a gown since I graduated, and I had even less experience walking in high heels. My somewhat forced smile became genuine when I saw Matt. The man was heart-stoppingly gorgeous in his tuxedo. He stared at me as I walked, like he couldn't take his eyes off me. He was such a dear friend, and I loved him so much. I knew having him by my side today would help tremendously. As the maid of honor, I was officially paired with Brady's brother for the day. That would only be for official dances and stuff, though. Eric had a girlfriend, so he would be with her for the most part. I was grateful that Matt had come stag. At least I wasn't the only unattached member of the bridal party.

Matt smiled at me as I took my place near the altar. Emotional robot that he was, his small gesture meant a lot to me. Made me feel like Matt would be watching out for me the same way Brady would look out for Lyric.

After the cute little flower girl made her way down the aisle, the music swelled for the bridal entrance. Everyone stood to watch Lyric and her father proceed down the aisle. I could tell by the look on her face the moment she caught sight of Brady. Her tense expression softened, and she smiled.

That is what true love looks like.

As happy as I was for Lyric and as proud of her as I was for handling the stress of this moment with such grace, the ache in my chest sharpened. Watching a joyous bride, even one who was a dear friend, proceed down the aisle toward her husband-to-be was more painful than I'd anticipated. It hurt so much that I needed to turn away.

I caught Matt's gaze. He was still watching me, his expression nearly as pained as mine.

Locking eyes with me, he mouthed, "It's okay."

I nodded, my eyes filling with tears at his kindness. I fought those tears hard, willing myself not to cry. The thought of anyone pitying me was unbearable. Well, anyone besides Matt. I was okay with him feeling sorry for me for some reason.

Once Lyric had safely arrived at the front of the church, the bridal party sat. It was a relief to get off my feet and no longer be in front of everyone. All eyes would be on the bride and groom now, so I wouldn't have to fake it quite so much.

The ceremony was lovely, and Brady barely took his eyes off his bride. Matt barely took his eyes off me, and that helped more than he could ever know. It felt like I had a secret ally in my fight to survive the wedding without falling apart. He might be a man of few words, but sometimes you didn't need words to show support. Sometimes you just needed to be there for the people you loved, and I knew I could always count on him to have my back.

Lyric's parents, a professional music duo, performed during the wedding. They'd written the lovely song themselves, with sweet lyrics and a stirring melody. The fact that it was her mother and father singing and playing the guitar made the song even more moving. Lyric wiped her eyes the whole time they were performing, and I was grateful to be a part of such a special moment. For me, that was the highlight of the ceremony as it allowed me to feel a part of something beautiful that didn't make me feel lonely at the same time. If nothing else, it reminded me of how lucky I was when it came to family. My parents were wonderful, and I adored my brother, Jerry. And Matt was practically family as well. In spite of everything, I had a lot to be thankful for.

As the ceremony came to an end, I let out a deep sigh of relief. A sense of accomplishment washed over me as I walked back down the aisle of the church. It hadn't been easy, but I'd made it through the wedding without falling apart. There was still more to come—the after-wedding photographs, the dinner, and dancing—but I felt a little stronger now. It would all be over in a matter of hours, and I knew I'd never regret being a part of Lyric's special day.

I headed for the bar as soon as I got to the reception. Though I had no intention of getting sloppy drunk, I was eager to have some alcohol to take the edge off. I usually drank beer, but I was dressed up and feeling classy, so I opted for wine for once. It hit my empty stomach quickly, and a warm calm spread over my body. Tempting as it was to dull the pain, I'd seen enough drunken bridesmaid videos online to scare me into keeping my wits about me. Heartbreak plus too much wine equaled humiliating online infamy. No thanks. I'd have plenty of time to get hammered later in the safety of my own home.

I'd managed to keep a solid buzz going without over-doing it by the time the bride and groom arrived after the cocktail hour. When Mr. and Mrs. Keaton were first intro-duced in the banquet hall, we all stood up and cheered their arrival. My spirits lifted just hearing the celebration erupt all around me. Such a good group of friends were gathered here, and there was something so heartwarming about everybody coming together with joy and laughter. I smiled to think that, soon enough, it would be Mr. and *Dr.* Keaton, thank you very much.

Once we were seated, Brady's brother got up from our table to give his best man's speech.

"A lot of people, including me, never thought the day would come when Brady Keaton settled down," Eric began. Laughter and nods from the crowd greeted that statement. "Standing here, it's hard to believe that the dapper guy in the tux is the same one who used to wear his underwear as a hat."

That got even more laughter, including from Brady.

"Even just a few years ago, I don't think any of us could have imagined that he would take a bride. After all, this is the guy who used to party too much, drink too much, and make headlines for trashing hotel rooms."

Things got a little quiet after that uncomfortable truth.

"Hang on, I'm going somewhere with this," Eric said with a smile. "Everything changed when he met Lyric. That's what happens when you fall in love. Things change. You change. In this case, it isn't that Lyric made him change or forced him to calm down. Instead, she *inspired* him to change. Because of her and her love for him, he wanted to be a better person."

Brady nodded and gently slid his arm around his new wife. She rested her head on his shoulder as she listened to Eric.

"Real love—the kind that endures—is what happens when you find someone who truly brings out the best in you. And I think we can all agree that is the kind of love we see here today. Brady and Lyric truly bring out the best in each other through their support, friendship, and selflessness. And I know that their love will endure the ups and downs of baseball, medical school, and all of life's other challenges. And now, if you will join me in raising your glass." Eric paused for a moment so the guests could join the toast. "Here's to my big brother," he said, his voice cracking with emotion, "and my new sister-in-law. Wishing you a long life filled with love and friendship. You sure hit a home run when you met this one, dude."

"Hear, hear!" Angel shouted as everyone clinked glasses.

Love and friendship. That's what it was all about, wasn't it? Once upon a time, Kyle had been my best friend. Seemed like a long time ago now.

After the toast, Brady and Lyric shared their first dance together. They'd chosen "The Power of Love" by Celine Dion. The tenderness between them and the emotions the romantic music stirred up hit me hard. Letting out a weary sigh, I began to realize that the reception would be much tougher than the wedding. At least during the ceremony I been able to watch from the sidelines and mope silently. At the party, I was supposed to be upbeat and happy. I dreaded the many love songs I'd have to hear for the rest of the night.

For the second song of the evening, the bridal party was expected to join in on the dance floor. Eric smiled at me, offering me his hand like a gentleman. The last thing I felt like doing was dancing, but it was part of the maid of honor gig.

"You've done a great job helping Lyric with all this," Eric said, glancing around at the ballroom and then back at me as we danced together. "Brady says you've kept the bride calm, which is no easy feat."

I smiled, relaxing slightly. Eric was a nice guy who had a girlfriend, so there was no pressure in sharing a simple dance with him.

"Not like it was that hard. Lyric's not exactly a bridezilla."

Eric chuckled, and I could see the warmth in his brown eyes that resembled Brady's.

"No she's not. Thank God. I used to worry a lot that some gold digger might get her claws into him. Lotta women would have no problem spending all his money. I'm so glad he found somebody who loves him for real."

"Me too," I said with a smile.

Eric twirled me at the end of the dance, making me laugh. Being all dressed up and dancing with a handsome man felt good. This was probably the way the rest of the reception would go. Just like Eric had mentioned in his speech. Ups and downs. Times when I'd feel joy for the happy couple and plenty of moments of loneliness and despair. Good thing I didn't have to work tomorrow. I'd probably need the whole day to recover.

Dinner was served: a succulent prime rib with red potatoes. The food was delicious and eating something substantial gave me a boost of energy. I'd need that strength to get through the next few hours. Eric sat to my left, and I had Matt on my right. Having Matt close by with his watchful eye helped so much. He knew I was hurting, and he cared. How I adored him, now more than ever.

The reception wasn't all bad. I did love to dance, and the faster songs were a blast. During one number, I got out on the dance floor with Lyric, Jana, and Aunt Clara. The guests loved seeing the bridesmaids dance with the bride, and we whipped the crowd into a frenzy. It pulled me out of my sad pit of despair for a while. Every time I started feeling better, though, the band would play a slow, romantic ballad and burst my balloon all over again. Ups and downs. Joy and despair. *All night long.* It was physically and emotionally exhausting.

During one slow song, I retreated to my table and collapsed into a chair. I'd kept on my happy-bridesmaid face all night, and it was wearing on me. Just for a minute or two, I let myself look as forlorn as I felt.

"May I have this dance?"

I jumped, startled at the sound of Matt's voice. I saw that familiar worried expression on his face, but he smiled as he held out his hand to me. I didn't feel like dancing anymore, but I wasn't about to turn down the man who'd been doing his best to take care of me all night in his own silent but protective way.

"I'd love to," I said, taking his hand. As he led me to the dance floor, I realized that dancing with him was preferable to sitting and listening to yet another draining love song by myself.

"You're a knockout in that dress, Julia," he said, eying me appreciatively before pulling me close.

"Thanks," I said.

"Even so, I think you're even sexier in shorts or blue jeans. You're at your most beautiful when you're out on the field wearing a baseball cap and working hard."

That was when I felt the most like myself. Out working on the baseball field. I sighed. "You know me so well, Matt."

"You bet I do. How are you doing?" Matt's blue eyes were filled with concern as he asked me that loaded question.

"This is harder than I thought it would be," I said quietly.

"I can't imagine how much it hurts just being here right now. The timing couldn't be worse," Matt said grimly. "But you're doing great. You helped make this day perfect for Lyric and Brady. You're so strong, Julia."

"I needed to hear that," I whispered, pulling him closer.

"It's gonna be okay," Matt murmured in my ear.

Resting my head on his shoulder, I was deeply thankful that I had Matt to lean on, literally. My legs felt weak, like I didn't know how much longer I could keep being brave. After swaying to the music for a short while, I realized how much I needed to get some of this heavy weight off my chest.

"I never told you the truth about what happened between me and Kyle. I never told anybody."

I lifted my head to look at him. Gazing into my eyes, he nodded gently, encouraging me to continue.

"It wasn't mutual, like I told everybody it was. Kyle broke it off. I had no idea it was coming. I was *completely* blindsided."

My eyes filled with tears. I rarely cried, so Matt knew how devastated I felt.

"Oh Julia," he said softly, looking nearly as distraught as I was.

"He met somebody else." God, it hurt to say those words out loud.

Matt's muscles tensed as he held me.

"That son of a bitch," he said through clenched teeth. Matt's anger floored me. He was always calm and collected. I'd expected quiet sympathy, not fury.

"What?"

"What kind of guy proposes and then leaves you for somebody else? What the fuck is wrong with him?"

"I honestly have no idea." For the first time since we broke up, I felt angry instead of hurt. And it was a huge relief.

"Kyle is out of his fucking mind," Matt said, gripping me so hard it started to hurt. He winced when he realized what he was doing. Easing his grip, he said, "Sorry. Sorry! I'm just so damn mad. Only a lunatic would let you go, Julia. I hope you know that."

"You're sweet to say that," I told him, flattered that he was so angry on my behalf. Matt was such a good friend.

"It's true," he insisted.

"It's hard for me to believe that right now. I can't even begin to tell you how scary it is when the person you love most in the world just walks away from you. Believe me, it makes you question everything."

I let out a deep, weary sigh. Though I was glad I'd told Matt the truth, I was more emotionally wrung out than ever.

The romantic song ended, and Matt tenderly traced my cheek with his finger. He didn't say anything more, but he didn't need to. His strong, silent support spoke volumes.

Kyle might have bailed out on me, but I knew my dear friend Matt never would.

17

MATT

I'd kept a close eye on Julia throughout the entire wedding and reception. She was holding up pretty well, but I could see the emotional strain of the affair was taking its toll. I was glad I'd asked her to dance when I had. Not only had it felt amazing to touch her and hold her in my arms, it had given her a chance to talk about what had really transpired between her and Kyle.

Rage boiled inside me when I thought about it. That bastard had broken Julia's heart. I hadn't seen it coming, so I couldn't imagine how painful it must have been for her. I wanted to choke the living shit out of the guy, both for hurting her and for not realizing what he'd had with her. All this time I'd had to stand on the sidelines and watch him with Julia only to have him toss her aside. *What in the hell was that dumb fuck thinking?*

Now that I knew the truth, my heart ached even more for her. Everybody celebrating love with the happy bride and groom, nothing but romance as far as the eye could see. My teeth clenched and my muscles tightened just thinking about how rejected Julia must be feeling right now. It was so goddamned unfair. Any man would be lucky to have her, but I could tell she didn't know that. She'd always been popular, and I was sure there was a long line of men who would jump at the chance to be with her now that Kyle was out of the picture. No way was I the only one. Judging by the pain I saw in her eyes, Julia had no idea how much everybody loved her.

Julia stood with the other women during the bouquet toss, but she didn't even attempt to catch the flowers. And who could blame her? She probably couldn't imagine being the next one to get married, so might as well let some other girl grab the bouquet.

After the bouquet and garter tradition came the cake cutting. Smiling, Brady gently dabbed a finger full of frosting on his wife's nose rather than smash the cake in her face. Cake smashing was a dumb tradition I never understood. I knew how much work and expense went into the bride's hair and makeup, and why any groom would want to mess that up was beyond me. After feeding each other the cake, symbolically pledging they would never let the other go hungry, they shared a sweet kiss. I could not have been happier for my buddy. Across the room, Julia smiled sadly as she watched the bride and groom together. I thought of everything she'd endured today—the vows, the first dance, the toasts. All the things she was supposed to do in a few short months with her husband-to-be. My God, I'd never know how she made it this far with her broken engagement so raw and so recent.

I went to the bar to grab another beer. The party was still going strong. People were having a great time, and I was glad the wedding and reception had gone so well. After a few loud, upbeat songs to get people back out onto the dance floor, the band started playing another slow ballad. It was a deeply romantic song about knowing when you've found that forever kind of love. I sighed deeply, understanding exactly what the guy was talking about. I watched Angel and Jana dance slowly together, their arms around each other and gazing into one another's eyes. Then I scanned the room to find the girl I had loved forever.

My heart seized in my chest when I saw her standing in the back of the room, holding on to the wall like she was ready to collapse.

"Oh shit," I said, slamming my drink down on a nearby table and rushing over to her.

She had her hand over her mouth, desperately trying to hold back a sob. I had never seen her like this. It was horrible.

"Julia?" I said, alarmed.

She looked up at me, those hazel eyes filled with pure agony.

"This ..." she began shakily. "This song was supposed to be our first dance at our wedding."

"Oh God," I moaned, feeling utterly helpless, no idea what to do to ease her pain.

"I can't do this anymore," Julia whispered.

I nodded. She had reached her breaking point. It was time to go.

"It's okay," I told her. Pulling her into my arms, I held her close. She was trembling, and I had to fight the urge to pick her up and carry her out of there. But I knew my Julia. She didn't want anyone's pity. She had fought hard to get through this experience with dignity, and I intended to help her leave with her head held high.

"You've done a great job today, Julia. You were there for Lyric and Brady, and I know they will never forget that. But it's time for you to go home now and get some rest."

Lifting her head, she asked, "Will you take me home?"

"Yes. Of course I'll take you home. I'll take care of everything," I assured her.

"Thank you, Matt. Thank you so much. I couldn't have gotten through tonight without you." Her eyes were still filled with deep sorrow, but she had calmed down a little.

I spied Brady leaning on the bar, chatting with the bartender. I quickly headed over to him.

"Hey man," I said, clapping him on the back. "Need to talk to you for a sec."

"Everything okay?" he asked, stepping away from the bar so we could talk.

"Yeah, everything's okay," I said. "But I'm afraid I gotta get going."

"Really? Why?"

"I've got to get Julia out of here, man. She just ... I think she's had enough for one day."

Brady nodded grimly, getting my meaning right away. "I'm sure she has. She's been so great with Lyric through this whole thing, but it's gotta be so rough on her right now."

"Exactly. She's one hell of a trouper, but I want to get her home so she can rest."

"I understand completely. God, I hope she's okay."

Sighing heavily, I said, "She will be. Just gonna take some time. Listen, don't tell Lyric why we're leaving. I don't want her to feel bad about any of this."

"Right. I appreciate that," Brady said, clapping me on the back and then pulling me in for a hug. "Thanks, man. For everything."

"My pleasure. Congrats," I said with a smile.

"Oh hey, you should take the limo," Brady said.

"Really?"

"Yeah. Take it. We're not leaving any time soon, and the

guy's just sitting out there waiting. I'll ask him to meet you out front," Brady said, digging his cell phone out of his pocket.

"Great. Thanks."

I'd be able to take Julia home in comfort and style. More than anything, she needed to be somewhere private where she could stop pretending she wasn't utterly heartbroken. I couldn't imagine how exhausting that must have been for her.

I stood back at a respectful distance as she hugged Lyric and said her goodbyes. Julia was smiling, but I could see the concern on Lyric's face. She wasn't stupid. But she was gracious, hugging Julia warmly and thanking her for all her help.

I ushered Julia out of the ballroom as quickly as I could. Once the double doors were safely shut behind us, she let out a deep breath.

"You did great tonight, Julia. I'm really proud of you," I told her.

She nodded. "I'm just glad it's over."

Putting my hand protectively on her back, I led her toward the elevator. "Good news. Brady's lending us the limo."

"Oh, that's really sweet of him," Julia said.

I pressed the elevator button and we waited for it to arrive at our floor.

"Matt," she said. "I want you to take me home."

My brow furrowed, and I wondered if she'd had too much to drink. Unlikely, since I'd been watching her like a hawk all night and she hadn't imbibed much since the cocktail hour.

"I know, Julia. That's what I'm doing."

"No," she said, staring at me. "I want you to take me to *your* home. To your bed."

My eyes flew open wide. It wasn't easy to get a rise out of me, but when it happened, it was usually Julia who'd done it.

"What are you talking about?"

"I haven't been with a man since Kyle dumped me. I miss it. I miss sex."

I nodded. Julia had always had a voracious sexual appetite, and I'd often wondered how she dealt with the long stretches of abstinence that came with a long-distance relationship. Still, I couldn't believe what she was saying to me.

"Well, sure you do. But—"

"And I miss being touched," Julia said, the tremble back in her voice. "These last few weeks, and especially tonight, have been so hard, Matt. You have no idea."

Her hazel eyes were drenched in sadness, and she looked so distraught I could hardly bear it. It was dangerous, because I knew I would do just about anything to make her feel better.

"I need to forget for a while. Please, Matt," Julia pleaded. "Take me to bed and make me forget."

Her eyes filled with tears. I would never get used to seeing Julia Frederick cry.

"Julia, I—"

The elevator dinged and the doors slid open. Talk about being saved by the bell.

Dear God, I can't do this. Can I?

We stepped into the elevator, and I pressed the button for the lobby. My mind swirled with a million thoughts at once. Sex with Julia was a bad idea. The worst. For so many reasons.

For one thing, she might as well be drunk since she was so emotionally unstable that she wasn't thinking clearly. Having sex with any woman in that kind of state was just wrong.

And this wasn't just any woman.

This was the woman I loved. Taking her to my bed again might well destroy me. How would I ever treat her as just a friend once we got back to work? For years I'd had to pretend my heart wasn't ripping in half every time I saw her with Kyle. If we had sex now, it would be even tougher to pretend we were just pals from the old neighborhood every time I ran into her at Old Bay Stadium, which was *all the time.*

"Matt?" she asked after a completely silent elevator ride to the lobby.

We stepped out and off to the side where we could talk.

"Julia, this is crazy."

Tears spilling down her cheeks, she said, "I already feel like nobody wants me. Kyle rejected me, and I couldn't take it if you rejected me, too."

Good Christ, now what was I supposed to do? Not only was I trying to figure out what was best for her, my own resolve was weakening. *Of course* I wanted her. For years I'd dreamed of being able to touch her again. To hold her in my arms. To show her I was no longer the shy virgin she knew in college. Now I knew how to make a woman scream my name when I gave her what she needed. Oh yes. I could make Julia forget her pain for a while.

The question was ... *should I?*

"Of course, I'm not going to *reject* you," I said. Only fucking idiots like Kyle Nolan did stupid things like that.

"Good," she said. The relief that shone in her eyes told me I was in very big trouble. I couldn't do this ... but I couldn't *not* do this.

I'd thought my night with Julia in college had been my once-in-a-lifetime opportunity to be with her, and now she was giving me a second chance. But should I take it?

Sucking in a deep breath, I focused on the most important consideration in all this. *Julia.* I needed to figure out what was best for her. Quickly trying to weigh the pros and cons, I thought about what might happen in the future. Would she get hurt if we slept together? Or would it hurt more if I turned her down?

The sleek white limo slid up in front of the entrance to the hotel, and Julia let out a deep groan.

There, across the back of the limo, was a huge JUST MARRIED banner. Clearly, neither Brady nor I had thought this through.

Julia's beautiful eyes filled with fresh tears.

The driver stepped out of the limo and opened the door for us. He helped Julia inside and I slid into the car after her. After he returned to his seat up front, he asked, "Where to?"

I told him my address.

That made Julia smile.

God help me.

18

MATT

Julia and I rode in the back of the limo as it sped toward my place. For so long, I'd dreamed about making love to her, but now that it might actually happen, I was a complete wreck. In the fantasy version of our sexual escapades, Julia *wanted* me. She was as hot for me as I was for her, and we had wild sex for hours because we were a happy couple. The reality version featured a broken-hearted Julia desperate to use sex as a temporary escape from her pain.

"Would it really be so bad, Matt?"

"What?" I asked.

"Is the idea of having sex with me so terrible that you're ready to snap your own fingers in half?"

I followed her gaze and realized my fists were clenched tightly as I sat, stiff as a board.

When I looked up, the fresh pain in her eyes nearly broke me.

Forcing my tense body to relax, I touched her face. "Of course not. But you must understand the position you're putting me in, Julia. It feels like I'm taking advantage of you. You're not in an emotional place to think clearly."

Julia's face fell. "Oh my God," she said, suddenly going pale.

"What's wrong?"

"You wouldn't be taking advantage of me." She closed her eyes and let out a deep sigh. After quite some time, she opened them again. "I'm taking advantage of *you.* I'm putting you in an impossible situation, and it's not right. When a man pressures a woman like this, they call it emotional rape. And it's no different when a woman does it."

"Oh, sweetie. It's not like that."

Her eyes filled with fresh tears. "Yes, it is! I'm sorry I'm such a mess, Matt."

"You're allowed to be a mess every once in a while."

Julia Frederick was a strong woman. Always had been. But even strong people needed help sometimes. I had little doubt she would emerge from this breakup prouder and more fiercely determined than ever before. That would take time, though. She was at a low point right now, and she needed a boost.

"Look, let's just go back to my place now and we can talk. You're always taking care of people. Let me take care of you for a change."

She nodded, and then she snuggled close to me for the rest of the ride.

The driver pulled up outside of my apartment building. I got out of the car first and offered my hand to help Julia out. She looked so gorgeous in that gown, even if it wasn't exactly her style. I thanked the driver and gave him a generous tip before sending him on his way.

"Wow, this is some place you got here," Julia said when we stepped into my luxury apartment.

"Thanks," I said.

This place was nothing compared to my house in Pennsylvania, but it was rather fancy. With a large kitchen and three bedrooms, it was spacious for a bachelor pad. It wasn't far from the stadium, and it made for a comfortable place to be when I wasn't at the ballpark. Fortunately, the cleaning service had been by recently and the apartment was nice and tidy. I hadn't been expecting any visitors, least of all Julia Frederick.

"So much bigger than our place ... the one Kyle and I had in the off-season," she said, her voice trailing off. Today had been one thing after another to remind her of everything she'd lost.

New depths of despair and loneliness darkening her eyes. Julia desperately needed to feel desired, cherished, and loved.

"Come here," I said as I sat down on the couch and held out my hand for her. She nestled in against my body, and it felt like the most natural thing in the world.

I held her and stroked her hair for a few minutes.

Julia sighed heavily. "I hate this. I mean, not this! Not being with you. I mean—"

"I know what you mean," I said.

"Feels like nothing makes sense right now. All this time I thought Kyle loved me. Loved that I wasn't the super feminine type. That I was strong and loud sometimes, and that I love sports."

I nodded silently as Julia listed off all the things *I* loved most about her.

"And then he goes and leaves me for another woman

who seems completely different than me. Not that I really know much about her. Just saw a picture. But still ..."

"I understand," I said, hating the sorrow and confusion in Julia's voice. I hated that she was feeling so unbalanced, and that Kyle had rocked her self-confidence so badly. Julia was the most exciting, sweet, lovable badass I'd ever known, and more than anything, I wanted to remind her of all the reasons she *rocked*.

Julia was filled with sorrow, anguish, and uncertainty.

And I wanted to fix it.

Now.

"Do you still want to have sex?" I asked.

Julia sat up and looked at me, her eyes filled with surprise and a hint of amusement.

"Yeah," she said, eying me curiously.

"Then let's do it," I said, loud and firm so she knew I meant business.

"Are you sure?" Her expression was filled with cautious optimism.

Absolutely not.

And yet, just like all those years ago when she suggested sex on spring break, there seemed to be more reasons to do it than not. That colossal asshole Kyle had made Julia question her desirability, and *nobody* desired her more than I did. If I could make her feel like the sexy goddess she truly was, then I should go ahead and do it.

Of course, the selfish part of me couldn't help seizing the opportunity to have sex with her because I loved her so much. I never thought I would ever get the chance to make love to her again, and yet here she was, *asking* me to take her to bed.

Holding back would only hurt her. Besides, I didn't think

I was capable of holding anything back at this point. I wanted her, loved her more than she could possibly know. I might not be able to tell her that, but I could sure as hell show her.

"Yes. I'm game if you are," I said. Not exactly the sexiest way to seduce her, but I needed to make sure I got a clear "yes" from her before proceeding.

"You bet I am," Julia said in a husky voice. She was already sounding stronger and more like herself.

Needing no further invitation, I pulled her toward me and crushed my mouth to hers. My kiss was forceful and passionate, letting her know I was more than ready to give her what she needed. I'd hemmed and hawed enough, and the time for second-guessing was over.

Julia moaned as I kissed her, and her nipples were rock hard. There was nothing more exciting than having sex with a woman who was really into it. One who was practically crying out with sexual need. I was suddenly overcome with the desire to fuck her so hard she'd forget Kyle's name once and for all.

Between kisses, I managed to say, "Bedroom's down the hall."

"Let's go," she said breathlessly.

Grabbing her hand, I pulled her toward the master bedroom. When we got there, I let go of her hand and headed over to the nightstand next to the bed.

As I reached for the drawer, Julia said, "I'm on the pill."

"Good to know," I said with a grin.

Julia sat up straight on the bed, waiting for me to take charge.

"As incredible as you look in that dress, let's get it off you," I said.

Grabbing her hands, I pulled her to her feet and turned her around. She drew in a deep breath of anticipation as I slowly unzipped the back of her dress and let it fall off her. Julia was wearing a black lace bra and panty set underneath.

I turned her to face me and allowed myself a moment to admire her up and down.

"My God, you look breathtaking," I told her. Julia smiled gratefully at me.

"And you look so incredible in a tux that part of me wants you to leave it on while we do it," she said, hunger and sheer need in her voice. "Still, I think I'd prefer you naked."

Julia reached for my black bow tie, and I helped her take it off. I removed my jacket and tossed it aside, leaving the white shirt for her to remove at her will. She quickly went to work on my buttons, and it got me hard just watching how eager she was to get my clothes off. Like her, like *anyone*, I guess I needed to feel wanted and desirable, too.

After pulling off my shirt, she took a full step back to look at my chest.

"My God, Matt. Look at you!" she said, eyes wide. "I guess I knew you were in great shape, but you are *ripped.*"

As an athlete, naturally I worked out a lot. Being around Brady so much, sometimes I felt inadequate by comparison. Still, I was more jacked than the average guy. Kyle was an athlete, too, though. I pushed that thought out of my head.

Julia flung her arms around my neck and kissed me. Together, we got the rest of my clothes and shoes off. Once I was naked, she looked down at my cock, hard and ready for action.

"Oh Matt," she moaned. "I need you so bad. You have no idea how much."

Had it been any other woman, I might have teased her a bit before getting right down to it. But I wouldn't do that with Julia. Not this time. She needed sexual relief, and she needed me to help her forget everything for a while.

I pushed her down on the bed. Her eyes flashed with excitement, and it was then that I knew I was doing the right thing. At last, she was focused on something other than heartbreak.

I slid my hands underneath her panties and pulled them off. When I reached under her back, she lifted herself up so I could unclasp her bra. My cock pressed against her, making her moan with need.

Kneeling before her, I grabbed her ankles and opened her up wide.

"Matt," she said breathlessly, her eyes wide with raw desperation. The *good* kind of desperation this time. The kind I could fix by slamming my cock into her. Waiting only a second more, I did just that.

Julia let out the sexiest, most sensual deep groan.

"Oh God, that's good!" she cried out.

I stopped kissing her for a moment so I could plant my hands on the mattress near her head and thrust in and out of her as hard as possible. Arching her back, she cried out my name over and over again. Talk about a dream come true. Every time I had jerked off thinking about her, I'd fantasized about her screaming my name.

I grabbed her right leg and flung it over my shoulder so I could penetrate her deeper. Not only was sex with Julia thrilling and deeply pleasurable, I reveled in being able to show her how far I'd come since our first tentative night so long ago. After I got the bed rocking hard, the headboard slamming against the wall, I pulled out of her.

"No!" she cried. "Matt, please. You can't tease me like that. Not now."

Julia Frederick was in my bed begging me to satisfy her. This was positively *surreal,* and I had no idea what I'd done to deserve this incredible experience.

"Don't you worry," I said, staring into her eyes. "I'll take care of you. I'm gonna lick you 'til you scream."

She drew in a breath and nodded, her eyes wide. I was always intense, but this was on another level. And she knew it. What she didn't know was she brought it out in me. Julia was so sexy and beautiful it made me feel out of control. And I loved every second of it.

Positioning myself between her legs, I tongued her most intimate spot. Yet another important lesson I'd learned over the years—how to *really* satisfy a woman.

Julia's breath came in gasps in between cries of my name. Over and over, she pleaded with me not to stop. Based on her whimpers, I figured out the perfect rhythm to bring her to her peak.

When she reached orgasm, she let out that same husky cry of bliss she'd cried out when I first slammed into her. When her climax finally subsided, she ran her fingers through her luscious curly brown hair.

"Matt," she said in a deliciously exhausted, sexually satisfied voice. "I've never come that hard in my *life*."

It was music to my ears, as was her orgasmic cry that was far louder than the first time I made her come, all those years ago. I could only give her a few seconds to bask in post-orgasmic bliss because I badly needed to join her in that state before I exploded. I slid back inside her, and Julia lifted her right leg and put it back on my shoulder. I guess she liked that position, and I found that sexy as hell.

"Julia, Julia," I said, riding her hard again. I was close ... *so close* ... "You're so beautiful it makes me *crazy*. Julia, Julia ..." With a sound that could only be described as an animal-like roar, I came hard inside her.

Still groaning with sexual relief, I pulled out of her and collapsed beside her. My body tingled all over; it had been a long time since I'd felt this good. No matter how many other women I'd been with over the years, Julia was still the only one I really wanted.

"You've learned *a lot* since college," Julia said, sounding sleepy and satisfied.

"You're pretty hot yourself. You're so damn sexy, you drive me wild, girl."

"Thanks," she said uncertainly. I knew she didn't believe me.

Slipping my arm underneath her shoulders, I pulled her close to me. I didn't typically like to cuddle after sex, but this was Julia. I couldn't pass up any opportunity I had to touch her.

"Everything's gonna be okay," I said, stroking her hair tenderly.

Holding on to each other, we dozed off a bit. Well, at least she did. I was tired, but I didn't want to fall asleep and miss one second with her. All too soon, this experience would be over, and I would have to go back to pretending she was just a friend and coworker.

I hadn't realized she'd woken up until she said, "You up for another round?"

"Seriously?" I asked, my cock already twitching in response.

"I'm game if you are," she said with a wink.

Once was not enough. Twice wouldn't be enough, but I would take whatever she was willing to offer me.

"I can help you get ready," she said.

"What do you mean—" Before I could even finish my sentence, Julia's mouth was around my cock. "Ohhh."

I closed my eyes, surrendering to Julia's power over me. Getting a blow job was pretty high up on my long list of fantasies about her. Good thing I'd already had an orgasm not too long ago, or this would have been the shortest blow job ever.

"Okay," I croaked. "You got me ready all right."

It was killing me to tell her to stop, but I'd never make it back inside her if she kept doing this to me. Julia took her mouth off me and it took all my resolve not to beg her to keep going. She had other plans anyway.

Julia straddled me and then slowly, sensually slid herself down my cock, moaning as she did so. I loved having her in this position since it gave me a full view of her glorious breasts. She ground herself against me, and I watched her face contort with pleasure. This girl was so uninhibited in bed. She knew what she wanted, and she also knew how to give me pleasure beyond my wildest dreams.

What the hell was Kyle Nolan thinking?

I already recognized the noises Julia made when she was about to come. She moved her body against my cock in the perfect rhythm to reach her peak and fast. Fascinated, I watched her buck and thrust, her pleasure visibly growing in intensity with each move she made. She ran her hands over my muscles and my ego soared as her eyes grew wide with deeper arousal.

Julia Frederick is hot for me. I can't believe this is really happening.

"Matt ... oh ... ah ..." She threw her head back and let out a husky, orgasmic cry of ecstasy.

"Sorry," she said breathlessly. "I should have waited for you."

"It's okay," I told her. Though her pleasure was more important than my own, I still needed to come. *Badly.* My arousal had been supercharged by her performance.

She lay down on the bed.

I sat up, looking down at her with renewed intensity.

Through clenched teeth, I said, "I want you on your knees."

Julia drew in a sharp breath. Then she whispered, "Yes."

I'd been so commanding, I'd half expected her to say *Yes, sir.*

She turned over and got down on all fours, offering herself to me. I took just a second to appreciate this momentous occasion. Once again, I asked myself what the hell I had done to deserve this incredible experience. But this was no time for questions. It was time for action.

I rammed into her from behind, earning another delicious cry from Julia. Thanks to my earlier release, I lasted a lot longer than I would have expected considering how fucking hot this was. Thrusting fiercely, I was a tad worried about being too rough, but judging by her cries of passion, she enjoyed the punishment I gave her lady parts. Too caught up in the moment, I pulled her hair.

"Matt," she said, her voice sounding strained.

Shit. That was too far for her comfort.

Before I could let go of her hair, she pleaded, "Reach around and stroke me. I'm so close. Oh Matt, I'm gonna come again."

Wow. Just when I thought sex with her could not possibly get any hotter.

I slid my hand around her front and found her clit. I stroked and she screamed. Then, in one perfect moment that I thought could only happen in a carefully choreographed X-rated movie, we both came at the same time. I kept rubbing her clit, making sure she finished coming while I emptied myself into her with a deep groan.

We both collapsed onto the bed, breathing heavily.

"No man has *ever* made me come three times in one

night," Julia said dreamily. "You are so much better than Kyle in bed. No contest."

I wanted to punch my hand in the air in triumph. Julia had no idea how much I needed to hear that after all these years of feeling jealous and inferior to that bastard.

I pulled her close and held her tenderly just as I had earlier. She snuggled up next to my bare skin, and I could honestly say this moment was one of the highlights of my entire life.

"I need this so much, Matt," she said. "In every way. Thank you."

"You know I'm always here for you, Julia," I told her softly.

"Yes. I do know that."

I didn't want to surrender to sleep, but I was mentally, physically, and emotionally spent. I couldn't hold out any longer, but at least I fell asleep with Julia cradled in my arms.

I finally woke up at around 10am or so. Julia was still asleep, so I got to have a few minutes to gaze at her while she lay beside me. It was a relief to be able to look at her with unabashed love rather than having to wear that constant poker face. I was tempted to whisper *I love you*, but it was too risky. I knew a lot of things about Julia, but I didn't know whether she was a light sleeper or not. After all, this was the first time I'd had the privilege of sharing a bed with her for the whole night.

Sure enough, she woke up.

"Hey," she said, sleepily stretching out her arms and smiling. I didn't see any hint of regret on her face, which was a relief.

After kissing my cheek, she got up to go to the bathroom. She was still naked, which I thoroughly enjoyed.

I heard the toilet flush, and then I heard the sound of her splashing water on her face. When she came back out, she stopped at the foot of the bed and looked down at the floor. Her face fell.

"What's the matter?"

Picking up her dress from last night, she grimaced. "I am such a sad, pathetic bridesmaid cliché right now."

"No you're not," I said.

"Yes, I am. Lonely spinster maid of honor begs groomsman to have sex with her after a wedding."

"It's not like that," I said, trying to think of a reason why she wasn't a cliché. I faltered, unable to come up with anything.

The look of despair was back, though less severe than it had been yesterday. Great sex was an excellent distraction, but it couldn't cure everything.

"Are you hungry? I can make you some breakfast."

After impressing her with my sexual prowess, I wanted to show off my cooking skills. Anything to prove to her I was boyfriend material.

"That's okay. I think I just need to go home and be alone for a while."

I'd known this moment was inevitable, but my heart was crushed all the same.

"Is that okay?" Julia asked, her eyes filled with concern as she looked at me.

Poker face, poker face.

"Of course," I said, getting out of bed. Julia seized that opportunity to take a long look at my naked body, which made me feel a little better. Maybe she would touch herself later and think of me.

Still naked, she grabbed her phone. I watched as she

pulled up a ride-sharing app. She was really leaving. I didn't even have the chance to offer her a ride home.

I understood she needed to be alone right now, and it was best to give her space.

Standing up, she made a face at the bridesmaid's gown again.

"You don't have to put that back on," I said. "I'm sure I can scrounge up something to fit you."

I headed toward my closet, hoping she was still looking at my nude body while I had my back to her. I got dressed before searching for something for her to wear home. I was so much bigger than her, but I did find some stuff that would fit.

"Here," I said, handing her a Baltimore Bay Birds shirt and a pair of drawstring shorts that she could at least tighten up around her waist.

"You're a lifesaver," Julia said. She put on her bra and panties and slipped my clothes on.

"You look amazing."

"Thanks," she said in a tone that meant she thought I was humoring her.

"I mean it," I insisted. "You never look sexier than you do when you're in a baseball shirt and shorts or jeans. You look like *you*, and I find that sexy as hell."

Julia graced me with a genuine smile. "Thank you, Matt. You always seem to know just what I need to hear."

All too soon, her ride showed up and she had to go.

It hurt like hell to say goodbye. I would see her at work soon, but that would be in a totally different capacity. I knew what had happened in my apartment would stay in my apartment. That was how it had to be.

"Take care of yourself, you hear me?" I told her as she headed toward the door.

"I will," she said. Then she turned around to face me. She had tears in her eyes, and it tore me up inside.

"Oh, Julia," I said, rushing toward her. I tenderly touched her face.

"No, no. I'm okay. Really." She gazed up into my eyes, and in a voice that was barely a whisper, she said, "Thank you for making me feel beautiful."

Tears spilling down her face, she blew me a kiss. And then she was gone.

19

JULIA

I arrived at Old Bay Stadium after the All-Star break feeling slightly unsteady. It had been such a whirlwind few days with my emotions running high. I'd allowed myself to sleep in a bit today, hoping to ease back into work. Rather than arrive super early before everybody else, I showed up around 10am. A smile spread across my face as I gazed out at the field that I loved so much. My crew was hard at work readying the field for the first game back after the break. It felt like Act II of the baseball season. In fact, it felt like Act II of my life. Like a do-over. And I was surprisingly okay with that. Not that I had a choice in starting over in my personal life, but I could choose how I responded to the curve ball life had thrown at me. I'd wallowed in self-pity for a while because that's what I'd needed to do. Now I was ready to start the healing process.

In a weird way, the wedding had probably helped with that. I'd been thrown into a difficult situation and I'd survived it. It hadn't been easy, and it sure wasn't pretty, but I'd done it. And I was ready to move on.

Watching my guys mow the outfield lawn and spray down the infield with water, I realized a few things.

I was good at my job, and I was good with people. I treated my crew well while still demanding excellence, and I knew they respected me.

I was a good person.

The fact that I wasn't good enough for Kyle should have nothing to do with my self-esteem. Right now, I needed to learn how to be single and be comfortable in my own skin before I could even think about another relationship. I was beginning to feel better, but still. My confidence, along with the foundation of my life, had been rocked. But I would feel strong again in time.

Overall, it wound up being a good day. Being so busy at the ballpark lifted my spirits. It also didn't hurt that I was utterly sexually satisfied, thanks to Matt. Holy hell was he good in bed. I could still feel a tingling between my legs where his cock had repeatedly rammed into me. He'd made me feel so desirable, and I loved the way he'd touched me. His strong hands had caressed me all over in a way that was deeply sexual but tender at the same time.

Perhaps our night of fabulous sex had been just what he'd needed, too, because his hitting had improved in tonight's game. He went 2 for 4 with three RBIs, and even when he got out, he looked good. Confident, like he was getting his swing back. I was so happy for him. I knew how much his batting slump was hurting him.

Matt wasn't the only one hitting well in tonight's blowout win against the Los Angeles Lions. Brady hit a grand slam in the eighth inning. The crowd went *insane*, and it was one of the most thrilling moments I'd had this season. The crowd energized me as the air crackled with electricity and excitement. There was something beautiful about a huge gathering of strangers cheering in support of the home team. One of the things I loved about sports.

I was struck by a strange sense of relief that I wouldn't have to tell Kyle about my day. After being on such a high from a great game, his underwhelmed reaction would have taken the wind out of my sails. It was awful the way he'd constantly minimized my life and the things that were important to me.

Being named head groundskeeper for a major league ball club was a *very big deal*, and how dare he act like it wasn't? Once again, it felt good to be mad instead of hurt.

As I hosed down the dirt after the game, I imagined what Kyle would have said if I'd told him about Brady's stellar performance, and it occurred to me that he didn't like hearing about other people's successes. This was especially true when it came to baseball. Now that I really thought about it, many of our relationship problems had started when I got this job.

Oh my God, I think Kyle was jealous of me.

He couldn't stand the thought that I'd made it to the majors before he did.

That thought both infuriated me and broke my heart. Couples were supposed to support each other. I would have been thrilled for Kyle if he had made it to the majors, because I knew how hard he'd worked for it and how much it meant to him. Looking back on his reaction to finding out I'd gotten my dream job, I realized his first inclination was to think about how my good news affected him. His selfishness had put a damper on one of the most important moments of my life.

Seriously, *screw* that guy.

Understanding the problems between us and figuring out why we'd broken up wasn't a miracle cure for my pain, but it helped. I still missed Kyle, and I mourned for a future that I no longer had with him. But I was feeling stronger now. Like I really would be okay.

As I headed back toward the clubhouse, I saw Matt standing on the warning track, watching me. My heart thudded in my chest when I caught sight of him.

Wow. That was new.

Usually when I saw Matt, a feeling of friendly affection washed over me along with the occasional stirring of arousal between my legs. I had always found him attractive, after all. But this feeling was ... different. It caught me off guard.

"How are you feeling?" Matt asked, eying me with concern.

I gazed at him fondly. He was always so sweet, and he was way more attuned to my emotions than Kyle had ever been.

"Pretty good, actually. Much better than the last time you saw me."

I felt a bit awkward remembering how weepy I'd been when I left his place after we'd spent the night together. The feeling passed quickly, though. I felt safe with Matt. Always had. And I knew he didn't think I was sad and pathetic. I'd been through a lot, and I'd been upset for a good reason.

"You did great tonight," I said, fist bumping him and pretending my knees hadn't suddenly gone weak when he looked into my eyes.

This was so weird. Matt was one of my best friends. I wasn't used to seeing him this way. I guess part of it was now I knew what an incredible lover he was. He'd been amazing, taking charge in bed. Matt was intense anyway, so I shouldn't have been surprised that his intensity had carried over into the bedroom. The whole experience had just been so wildly different from our first time together, when I'd had to guide him.

"Thanks," he said, his smile reaching all the way to his eyes. He must have been relieved to finally snap out of his batting slump. Sometimes all it took was one good night at the plate to turn things around after a bad run.

Normally after a game I would only chat with Matt for a few minutes if I ran into him at all. Then we would go our separate ways for the night. I suddenly realized I didn't want him to go.

"Do you want to go grab a drink?" I blurted.

"What?"

"Let's go grab a drink before we call it a night. It was such a great game tonight, and I'm still all hyped up. I don't think I'll be able to sleep right away."

Matt nodded. "Yeah, I get that way too sometimes. Sure, why not?"

Matt got changed and we headed out to a bar within walking distance of the ballpark in downtown Baltimore. There were likely to be Baltimore Bay Bird fans there drinking after the game, but that was okay. Matt was recognizable, but not nearly as famous as Brady. He wouldn't get mobbed by fans like Brady did everywhere he went.

"I owe you a drink for putting up with me," I told him as we walked into the bar. "For real, Matt. You took good care of me. I mean, *real* good care."

Matt blushed slightly, clearly getting my meaning. I laughed when I saw that. Funny how he could take charge and do things like order me to get on my knees in the bedroom and then blush about it later. He was adorable.

We chose a table toward the back of the crowded bar, and I ordered the drinks to minimize the fuss over him. It was like a game to see how long it would take the baseball fans to realize the second baseman for the Baltimore Bay Birds was in their midst. I chuckled to myself as I glanced at the big screen TV over the bar that featured the highlights from tonight's game.

"Oooh, I love your nails," I said to the bartender as she prepared our drinks.

"Thanks," she said with a bright smile, glancing at her sparkly purple nails that had obviously been professionally done. I'd only had my nails done in a salon once in my life, and that was for my high school prom. It was definitely not my thing, but I knew lots of women who went to great expense to keep their nails pretty, and I enjoyed making them feel good by noticing. Complimenting a woman's nails never failed to make her smile, and I loved that.

"Great game tonight, huh?" she asked, gesturing at my Baltimore Bay Birds shirt.

"Yeah, it was," I said with enthusiasm.

"You were there, I take it?" she asked.

I nodded happily, pleased to get the opening I wanted. "Yeah, I work there. I'm the head groundskeeper."

"No kidding," the lady said, her light brown eyes opening wide. "You take care of the grass and stuff?"

"Yup." I took the two beers she handed to me.

"That is very cool," the woman said with a smile.

"Thanks," I said with a nod.

I set our beers down on the table and took a seat across from Matt. He sat with his back to the front door of the place for anonymity purposes.

Matt grinned at me.

"What?" I asked.

He glanced over at the bar and then back at me. "You make friends wherever you go. Always have. I always liked that about you."

"Thanks," I said, feeling genuinely touched. Looking back, I recalled Kyle's frequent impatience while I chatted with strangers.

Matt lifted his mug at me and smiled before taking a sip. A shiver of delight rippled through me when he smiled.

This is just too weird.

I took a long drink and sat back in my chair, reveling in the relaxation of both the alcohol and being with Matt. I'd wanted to spend time with him after the game tonight both because I was craving the comfort of his presence and because a part of me kinda hoped we'd wind up in bed again. And yet, I wasn't sure I wanted to be friends with benefits. Both times we'd gone to bed had been because of a specific reason. The first time he'd wanted to lose his virginity and the second time I'd needed comfort and distraction from my painful breakup. We'd been there for each other in time of need, but out here in the real world, things could get complicated. I was never one to get super emotional about sex, but I was starting to worry I might be catching feelings for Matt. My head was still kinda messed up, and it was hard to tell if I was really into him or if I was just lonely and sad. The last thing I wanted was to treat my dear friend as a rebound guy.

"You look like you're doing better, Julia."

"I am, you know? I really am feeling a lot better. Like I told you, it was all such a shock at first. And Matt," I said, lowering my voice even though nobody in the place was paying any attention to us. "Nobody else knows that Kyle was the one to dump me."

"I know," he said, sympathy in his voice. "I won't say a word."

"I know you won't," I said. The idea of Matt being a gossip was ridiculous, but I wanted to be sure he didn't say anything. He was a man of few words anyway, so it wasn't like he would discuss my personal life with anyone.

"But it's like now that the shock of it all is starting to wear off, I've really had time to think about stuff."

"Like what stuff?"

"Like maybe things between me and Kyle weren't quite as good as I'd thought."

Matt nodded thoughtfully as he sipped his beer.

"Everything was about him. I did my best to support him through thick and thin. Looking back, I don't think he was there for me the same way. Like at first, he acted like my getting the job with the Bay Birds was no big deal."

"He what?" Matt asked so loudly that it startled me for a second.

"Yeah," I said with a bitter laugh. "I mean, it's not like he said it was no big deal, but he was clearly underwhelmed, and it sucked the joy out of it for me. I'm still kinda mad about that."

Fresh anger boiled as I recalled practically dancing around the apartment with excitement until Kyle came home and ruined the moment.

"To be fair, he did take me out to celebrate. He came around eventually. But to tell you the truth, I think he was jealous that I made it to the major leagues before he did."

Matt shook his head, looking seriously annoyed. And it made me feel vindicated to have him on my side.

"Do you know he actually said he felt better when you were in a batting slump?"

"You're kidding," Matt said, getting more visibly angered by the minute.

"Yeah. Can you imagine? Oh, I was pissed, believe me. I think that made me madder than his reaction to my getting the job. Since he's still struggling in the minors, Kyle said it made him feel better that he wasn't the only one having problems. You would never do that sort of thing, Matt. And you never treated me bad, even when you were in a terrible slump. You were still so supportive of me and my job when everything was going well for me."

I took time to think about that for a moment. How hard that must have been.

"It always made me sad to see guys struggling at the plate," I said. "Happened all the time in the minors. I've seen what it does to a guy. Tears 'em up inside. The fans booing them like they were sucking on purpose. Like the guy wouldn't give anything he had if he could only snap out of his horrible slump."

"That's exactly what it feels like," Matt said, and I could hear the hurt in his voice.

I shook my head. "No matter what I was going through in my life, I can't imagine having someone else's suffering make me feel better."

"Me neither."

"You're so sweet, Matt."

"Thanks," he said, sipping his beer. "I try."

Gazing at him and stifling a groan, I realized there was no question about it. Matt was sexy and dreamy and wonderful, and I was quickly seeing him slide out of the friend zone and into boyfriend territory. And that was bad, even dangerous, territory for me. My heart had just been crushed, and I had no interest in diving into another relationship so soon. Not only that, but Matt had never shown any romantic interest in me. If you didn't count the whole having sex thing, anyway. But that was just sex and not romance. Worst of all, I knew damn well that Matt was still hung up on the woman from college who'd broken his heart. Even if, by some miracle, Matt and I did become a couple, it could never work out. Sooner or later, he would realize I couldn't measure up to that woman who still had his heart. Then he would dump me just like Kyle had.

I couldn't go through that again.

Which meant Matt and I could only ever be just good friends.

Somehow, I would have to learn to live with that.

"Excuse me."

I looked up to see a man in his thirties or so tentatively approaching our table. I smiled at him, nonverbally giving him the go-ahead to interrupt us so he could fawn over Matt.

"So sorry to bother you," the guy said, glancing at Matt.

"No problem," Matt said.

"Would you mind?" The man took off his Baltimore Bay Birds cap and handed him a pen.

"Oh sure, man."

Matt signed his name with a flourish in large letters across the front of the cap. The baseball fan grinned ear to ear.

Then the guy turned to me. "And you. You're the head groundskeeper for Old Bay Stadium, right?"

I blinked at him, astonished. "Yeah. How did you know that?"

"Well," he said sheepishly, "I could lie and say I recognized you, but the truth is the bartender tipped me off. That's what made me look over here, and then I saw Matt Jovey."

I laughed. "Oh, okay. That makes sense."

"But for real, I do think I've seen you on TV, and you look a little familiar," the fan said with a smile.

It was true. They did show me on TV sometimes at the end of the inning when I brought my crew out. And Lyric told me that one time, one of the announcers laughed and said, "It's never a good sign when you see Julia Frederick studying her iPad intensely." He'd been referring to the dark storm clouds gathering and that if I was carefully watching the weather, it meant the game could be delayed. I hadn't thought much about it before, but I guess hardcore Baltimore Bay Birds fans that watched the games daily might actually know who I was. How cool was that?

After the fan walked away, Matt and I chatted for a while. We finished our beers and went our separate ways.

Still just friends.

20

MATT

After a lukewarm homestand where we'd won three games and lost four, we were off on an extended road trip to Seattle and Los Angeles. We had a rough outing in our first game in a four-game series against the Seattle Sailors, so Brady and I decided to grab a drink at a local bar. Neither of us had performed well tonight at the plate, and we'd managed to botch a double play that wound up costing us several runs. A stiff drink was definitely in order.

Though people recognized Brady everywhere we went, he was less likely to get mobbed by fans this far from Baltimore. It was safe to have a drink or two in public without causing too much of a scene. Brady loved the recognition anyway, especially after an off night at the ballpark.

"So you and Julia have been pretty chummy lately around the field," Brady said after we'd settled in with our beers at the bar. "More than usual it seems."

I shrugged and gulped half my beer in one swig. I'd been looking for an opening to talk about her with Brady, and it looked like this was it.

"There's rumors about you two, you know."

"No. I didn't know. Like what kind of rumors?"

"People just wonder if you two are an item, that's all. Everybody knows you've been good friends for a long time. That you go way back from before Julia started working with the Bay Birds. I guess nobody thought anything of it while she was engaged."

I drank more of my beer and nodded. "Oh. Makes sense I guess."

"You guys are still just friends, right? I mean, you would tell me if things were different, wouldn't you?" Brady asked, eying me curiously.

"I would. You'd probably be the first one I would tell."

"Good," he said with a smile. Knowing Brady, he would be offended if I didn't confide in him. Not only did the man love good gossip, but he was the only one in the world who knew how I felt about Julia.

"We are just friends, but ..." I began uncertainly.

"But what?" he asked, mug in hand.

"We slept together after your wedding."

"You what?" Brady slammed his mug down on the bar top so hard the liquid sloshed all over. He winced, realizing how loud he'd just been. "Sorry. But what the hell, Matt? You're just telling me this now?"

"Hey, be glad I told you at all. Nobody else knows. At least I'm pretty sure nobody else knows. Listen, you can't tell anybody about this. I mean it."

"I won't. I swear."

"Not even Lyric," I insisted. "*Especially* Lyric, actually. She and Julia are good friends. If Julia wants to tell her about it, she will. But it's not my place to say anything."

"Got it," Brady said with a firm nod. I knew my secret

was locked up tight in his vault. "So what the hell happened?"

I thought carefully about what to say. I felt a deep need to unburden myself, but I didn't want to betray Julia in the process. She'd been so vulnerable that night, worrying she was being a bridesmaid cliché.

"As you know," I began cautiously. "The wedding was tough on her."

"I know it was," Brady said, shaking his head sadly. "I can't tell you how grateful I am that she stuck it out for Lyric's sake. But I can't imagine how hard it was for her. I mean, the timing just couldn't have been worse."

"Exactly. Julia was just so sad that night, you know?"

"And she turned to you for comfort."

"Yeah, she did, but ... it's not as bad as it sounds. I mean, it's not like I took advantage of her or anything."

"Dude. That thought never even crossed my mind. You're not the type to manipulate any woman to get her into bed. And there's no way you'd ever do anything like that to Julia."

I nodded, relieved that Brady understood.

"You know how I feel about her. So of course, I wanted nothing more than to go to bed with her, but I was really worried about her getting hurt. We both knew exactly why she wanted to sleep with me. Like you said, she was reaching out for comfort."

Sipping his beer, Brady nodded as he listened.

"I thought about saying no. I really did. Julia was such an emotional wreck. She wasn't thinking clearly. It was like when a woman is super drunk and she's begging to go to bed with you."

"Yeah," he said nodding. "I get what you mean."

Brady had slept with a *lot* of women before he met

Lyric, but he never manipulated any of them to get them into bed. He might have been a playboy, but he was never cruel. Brady only took willing, perhaps buzzed but never drunk, women to bed. Any girl he'd slept with knew it was just for fun. Plenty of guys had no problem messing with a girl's heart just to get them into bed, but Brady wasn't like that. Neither was I, for that matter. I, too, had been with my share of women but I did my best to make sure nobody got hurt in the process. There was nothing wrong with safe casual sex, as long as everybody was on the same page about it. No attachments, no promises of the future. Just sex.

That worked out just fine, provided you weren't in love with the woman.

"For a lot of reasons, I knew having sex with Julia might be a very bad idea. But dude, she looked at me with tears in her eyes. She said she was already feeling so rejected by Kyle that she couldn't bear it if I rejected her, too."

I froze, realizing too late that I wasn't supposed to tell anyone that Kyle had been the one to break things off.

"Wow, that's rough," Brady said, not really taking notice of my slip.

Technically, I hadn't said that Kyle dumped Julia. I'd just said that she was feeling rejected.

Shaking his head, he said, "I mean, damn. What are you supposed to do when she says something like that?"

"Exactly. Even she realized she was putting me in an impossible situation, so she backed off the sex idea for a bit. She knew it wasn't right to pressure me into it. But the more I thought about it, the more I wanted to do it."

Brady chuckled. "Oh, I'm sure you did."

I laughed too. "Yeah, but it was more than just sex. It just made me so damn angry the way Kyle made her question herself. Made her feel unwanted. I needed to show her how desirable she really is."

"I get that," Brady said.

"Besides, Julia was never one to get all that emotional about sex. Before Kyle, she'd been with guys casually. I wasn't too worried that she'd be filled with regret in the morning. More than anything, she needed distraction. Just some no-strings sex to take her mind off her pain for a while."

Brady drained his beer and set the mug down on the bar. "And so far she seems to be okay with everything?" he asked.

"Yeah. Seems to be doing fine. Better, actually. I know she's still hurting, but the more time that passes, the better she seems to be handling the breakup."

Brady stared at me for a moment.

"What?"

"The question is, how are *you* doing?"

Right there, that question, was the reason I'd wanted to tell Brady about all this. He alone knew how much I loved Julia, and he understood the emotional toll that one night of allegedly "casual sex" might have had on me.

"It definitely messed with my head a bit," I confessed. "Having Julia around the ballpark all the time and knowing she belonged to somebody else really threw me off my game, both personally and professionally. I'm batting okay now, for the moment." Laughing, I said, "Well, if you don't count tonight."

Brady grimaced and nodded. He signaled the bartender for another beer, and I did the same.

"But I wonder what will happen if she starts dating somebody else," I said, my chest hurting at the mere idea.

"Yeah, that would be rough. But you never know, Matt.

Now that she's single, there's no reason why it couldn't work out between you two."

"I don't know. I'm pretty sure she just thinks of me as a friend."

"Wouldn't be the first time a friends-with-benefits thing turned into something more. Lyric and I started out that way."

"Really? I thought you started out by pretending you were a couple so the Baltimore owner would stop thinking of you as a drunken partier."

"We did. But during all those months of pretending, it wasn't like I could go bang some random woman like I used to, and Lyric couldn't sleep with anybody else either. So we figured we might as well enjoy the usual benefits of being a couple." Brady paused for a moment. "I remember how hard that was sometimes. We'd have sex in my bed, and then afterward she'd go and sleep in her own room because we weren't really together. For what it's worth, I understand exactly what you're going through, Matt."

I nodded appreciatively. It did help immensely, and it made me feel less alone.

"All that time, I was never sure if Lyric had feelings for me, but it turned out she did. For all you know, Julia feels the same way. I've seen the way she looks at you, Matt. There could be something there."

"She does love me. That much I know. Says it all the time. Always has."

Brady laughed. "Yeah. I get your point. She's said it to me, too."

I laughed along, feeling proud of Julia. "That's her way. She loves everybody, and she's not afraid to show it."

I thought about the night after the game when Julia and I had gone out for a drink. It made me smile, remembering how she had chatted with the bartender and been so warm and inviting to the fan who approached us. Julia exuded generosity and positivity, and her kindness was infectious. People always walked away from a conversation with her with big smiles on their faces.

Without even realizing it, I let out a deep, mournful sigh.

"I know, buddy. I know," Brady said sympathetically.

He did know. And that helped.

21

———

JULIA

As I carefully chalked the right field foul line for this afternoon's game, I reflected on how happy I was that my boys were finally back in town. I'd missed each and every one of them—some more than others, of course. I loved knowing Matt was close by, even on days when we both got too busy to talk to each other. I knew for sure I would see him tonight, though, since we had a dinner date scheduled.

Okay, so maybe it wasn't exactly a date. My brother and his boyfriend were in town, so we were all going out after the game. Since it was a Saturday afternoon, we had a big crowd in the ballpark. Weeknights were much slower, especially since the Bay Birds were down near the bottom of the standings. I was glad we had lots of people in attendance today, since this was an important day for me.

I'd done a brief interview with the Bay Bird's media team. It was one of those question-and-answer sessions they frequently did with the players, only it featured me talking about how I took care of the field before, during, and after the game. They would show it up on the jumbotron between the fourth and fifth inning. Once I'd mentioned my interview to my brother, he'd insisted on coming to the game.

It meant the world to me that Jerry and Parker would be in the crowd. I loved that I didn't have to tell my twin brother how important this interview was to me. He just knew. Yet another stark reminder of how important it was to have the people you love there to support you and how much it hurt when they didn't. Kyle probably wouldn't have made it to this game due to his own hectic baseball season, but I suspected he wouldn't have made much of an effort even if it were possible.

No. Kyle would *never* have gone out of his way to come to a major league ballpark where I would be the center of attention even if it was only for a few minutes. Shaking my head as I headed over to the left field line, I thought about how messed up that was. I understood how my success might be painful for him, but weren't you supposed to make sacrifices for the person you loved? Had it been me, I would have put aside my feelings of hurt and jealousy and cheered him on.

Today's debut of my interview was just one in an increasingly long list of important events in my life that Kyle was no longer around to ruin. I'd been with him for so long, I guess I hadn't noticed we weren't as happy together as I'd thought. Maybe I should give Kyle credit for paying more attention to the problems in our relationship than I had. He'd saved us years of unhappiness and a depressing divorce.

I shook my head again, eager to ward off the negative thoughts. Standing back to survey the beautiful land that was Old Bay Stadium, I inhaled a deep breath of the hot August air. A smile spread across my face, and my whole body tingled with happiness as I took in the smell of hot dogs, fried food, and freshly cut grass.

I could not love this job any more if I tried.

Game time finally arrived, and the crowd was positively teeming with good vibes. I giddily soaked it all in. The ceremonial first pitch was tossed by an adorable eight-year-old girl who was a cancer survivor. The crowd went wild for her, even after her pitch sailed well wide of the plate. I grinned as I watched a bunch of the Bay Birds, including Matt and Brady, enthusiastically high-five her as she giddily ran past them.

The Bay Birds were up 2-0 by the end of the fourth inning, and the fans in attendance still were in a good mood. At last, the time had arrived to show my interview up on the big screen. I was glad they had pre-recorded the interview, so I didn't have to worry about screwing up in front of all these people. Leaning against the warning track, I tried to pretend I wasn't screaming with excitement as I watched the jumbotron. My baseball cap and sunglasses helped me play it cool, I thought.

When the interviewer introduced me and said I was only the second female head groundskeeper in MLB history, the crowd cheered. I couldn't remember ever feeling so proud, and yet I was humbled to be part of something greater than myself. My eyes welled up as I thought of all the little girls in the stadium right now who were watching this. For all I knew, hearing my story might inspire some of them to follow in my footsteps.

The Q and A was only a few minutes long, but it was enough time for me to explain the basics of what the ground crew did every day. I was pleased with how it turned out. Brief and to the point, so as not to give people enough time to lose interest while they waited for game play to continue.

When it concluded, the announcer asked for a round of applause for Julia Frederick, head groundskeeper of Old Bay Stadium. The jumbotron then cut to a live shot of me, which I hadn't expected. Fortunately, I had the presence of mind to wave and tip my cap. The crowd clapped and cheered for me, and for the millionth time since I got this job, I wondered how in the hell I'd gotten so lucky.

How is this my life?

My heart soared as I drank in this perfect moment, made even more perfect knowing that Jerry, Parker, and Matt were here to witness this moment and that Kyle was *not* around to diminish it.

The Bay Birds went on to win 4-1, and I was thrilled that the game ended on a high note. I wrapped up my post-game work as quickly as I could, eager to go out with Jerry and Parker. And Matt, of course.

Jerry had thoughtfully suggested an Italian restaurant because he knew how much I loved pasta, so that's where we all met up after the game.

"That was the coolest!" Jerry said the moment he saw me walk into the lobby of the restaurant. He engulfed me in a bear hug, and I eagerly squeezed him back.

It was just a tiny, five-minute interview that only aired inside the stadium, but I loved that my brother treated it like it was a big deal. He was the best.

"Congratulations," Parker said, also giving me a hug. He was like an awesome bonus brother to me, and I was happy to have him with us to celebrate.

"Matt's not here yet?" I asked, surprised since he was usually able to leave the ballpark much more quickly than I could after a game.

"Oh, he's here all right. Big Shot's signing autographs," he said with a laugh and nodded in Matt's direction. I turned to find my favorite baseball player surrounded by a group of people who had recognized him.

"Poor guy," I said as I watched Matt patiently sign autographs and pose for selfies with fans. It was hit or miss when it came to getting cornered in public. Sometimes nobody noticed him and other times lots of people did.

Matt looked over, caught my eye, and smiled. My heart seized in my chest at the sight of him. I wondered if I would ever get used to reacting that way to him. It was still so new and strange. Matt was one of my dearest friends. He was my brother's best friend. And yet, it was like he'd gone from my old buddy to sexy, romantic hero practically overnight. I was still sorting through my churning emotions about him, and I wasn't sure what to make of it all.

For sure, I was not about to give Jerry any clue I was hot for his best friend, and he must *never* know that we'd had sex. Great sex. Fabulous sex. Multiple times.

"I'm starving," I announced, doing my best to kick naughty Matt thoughts out of my head. For now, anyway. There'd be plenty of time to indulge in those thoughts later when I was alone in bed. Lately, I'd especially enjoyed touching myself as I remembered how it felt to have my leg slung up on his shoulder while he pounded me senseless.

"Me too," Jerry said. "But they won't seat us until we're all ready."

I watched Matt politely disentangle himself from the small mob of Bay Bird fans. He dashed over to us with an apologetic look on his face.

"Sorry, I'm so sorry. Didn't mean to hold everybody up," Matt said before signaling to the hostess that we were ready.

"No big deal," I told him.

"It is a big deal," Matt said firmly. "This is supposed to be your night."

I smiled warmly at him, unable to resist tenderly touching his face. Matt was just so *different* from Kyle. I couldn't believe I'd never noticed it before. It occurred to me as we headed to the table what a nightmare Kyle would have been if he'd achieved fame on Matt's level while we were together. Or worse, if he ever became as famous as Brady. I could just see Kyle reveling in all the glory and attention, with visions of me standing alone at a hostess stand, hungry and waiting, while he entertained his legions of fans.

It wasn't that I didn't wish Kyle success, because I did. I was just relieved that I wouldn't be around to deal with it.

Matt pulled out my chair for me, and I stifled a dreamy sigh. Kyle never did things like that for me. For a split second, I felt bad for comparing Kyle to Matt. Then I remembered the bastard dumped me, so screw him.

We settled in our chairs and Matt immediately reached for the breadbasket.

"Carb-loading, are we?" Jerry teased.

"Shut your face," Matt said, taking a huge bite of bread.

I laughed. It was always fun to watch Jerry and Matt when they got together. Matt was usually cool and reserved, but he was more relaxed around his childhood friend.

Jerry reached for the breadbasket, but Matt snatched it away from him.

"Sooo hungry," Jerry said.

"Sucks to be you," Matt said. "Bread, Julia?"

"Why thank you," I said, gratefully accepting a roll and some butter.

Then I handed the basket to Parker. Jerry would eventually get some, but I didn't have to betray Matt in the process.

The waiter came by and took our order quickly, and I was grateful. The whole restaurant smelled of olive oil, garlic, and pasta, and I couldn't wait to sink into a great big plate of fettuccine alfredo. I didn't typically eat such heavy food, but this was a special occasion.

"That interview really was cool, Julia," Parker said. "Nice to see you get the recognition you deserve."

"Thanks," I said with a smile.

"Who knows? Fans might start to recognize you now," Jerry said.

"They already have," Matt said. "Even before the interview. Some guy at a bar the other night knew who she was."

Matt's blue eyes sparkled with pride as he spoke. He'd conveniently left out the part about the guy not exactly recognizing me, but that he'd been tipped off by the bartender.

"Oh, that's so wild," Jerry said, sounding impressed. "When people recognize me in public, they usually run away."

"That's because you're a dentist."

Jerry pouted sadly and nodded. "Nobody loves a dentist."

"*I* love a dentist," Parker said, making Jerry smile.

"Speaking of *love*," Jerry said.

"Jer." Parker shook his head. "You promised."

"I know I did," Jerry said in a whiny voice. "But this time is different."

Parker rolled his eyes, but he looked more amused than annoyed with my brother.

"I know this girl who would be perfect for you, Matt."

I fought to keep my expression calm and collected, even as I was tempted to tell Jerry to shut his mouth. I'd forgotten about Jerry's penchant for setting people up on dates, especially when it came to Matt. Scary thing was, my brother was quite good at matching people up. He was responsible for at least three weddings so far, and two of the couples were still married. Not a bad track record.

"Why do you keep insisting on setting me up, Jerry?" Matt asked. "Do you really think I have trouble finding dates? I do okay, you know."

More than okay. I was well aware that Matt had his fun while the team was away on road trips, but I tried not to think about it.

"I know you have no problem finding women to sleep with, dude," Jerry said. "But I'm not talking about one-night stands here. I'm talking about you finding a real relationship."

Matt sighed heavily and fiddled with his cloth napkin. I had the feeling he was lonely sometimes, and that made me sad.

"You've always said you wanted to settle down and have a family. That hasn't changed, right?"

"No. I guess not."

"Matt," Jerry said, sounding quite somber all of a sudden. "It's been what? Seven years now?"

"Seven years for what?"

"Seven years since that skank from college broke your heart."

"Don't call her that!" Matt snapped with such ferocity it made me jump. Whoever she was, that girl had really messed him up.

"I'm sorry. I don't mean to insult whoever this woman was," Jerry said, clearly annoyed at the person who'd hurt his friend so deeply.

"What the hell happened between you two anyway?" I asked.

"Don't bother asking," my brother said. "He won't tell us. Not a word. Believe me, I've tried."

"I just wish it had all gone down while I was still at college with him. I'd have given that girl a piece of my mind," I said.

Matt laughed. "I appreciate that, Julia."

Our food arrived, giving me a welcome distraction from discussing Matt's love life. The pasta was unbelievably good, and it tasted even better because I was so hungry. Taking a few minutes to eat while Matt and Jerry chatted about my brother's dental practice gave me time to think.

Mostly, I thought about how much I wanted Matt to be happy.

I'd come to think of him as so much more than a buddy. We already loved each other as friends, and we were definitely sexually compatible. Well, compatible wasn't even close to the right word to describe how mind-blowingly, explosively hot the sex had been. Combustible might be a better word. As much as I found myself longing to be with Matt romantically, he hadn't shown any interest in me that way. Just because I'd started seeing him in a totally different light didn't mean he felt the same way about me.

Jerry was right—Matt *had* always wanted to get married and have kids. Like playing professional baseball, it had been his dream for as long as I could remember. As much as it would hurt like hell to see him with another woman, I knew the right thing to do was encourage him to try to get over that woman from college and move on with his life. Even if it wasn't with me.

I tried to find comfort in the fact that now was no time for me to start a new relationship anyway. I was doing much better, but I was still emotionally unstable sometimes. All it took was hearing the wrong song on the radio and I fell to pieces. It happened less often now, but it still happened.

"You deserve to be happy, Matt," I said.

"What?" Matt asked, confused.

I'd been thinking so much about Matt's situation that I'd forgotten everybody else had moved on from the topic.

"Sorry. Just thinking about what Jerry said about setting you up with somebody. I think you should go for it."

"Really?" he asked. He seemed both surprised and sad when I said that.

Matt looked so hurt that I could barely stand it. I started to think "skank" wasn't a strong enough word to describe whoever had done this to him. I didn't usually have much of a temper, but right now I felt like bitch-slapping that woman for causing him so much pain.

"I know you're still hurting over that woman from all those years ago," I said, pausing as I tried to come up with the nicest way to say she wasn't coming back. "But I guess it just wasn't meant to be with her. And I hate the idea of you wasting any more time pining over some woman who clearly isn't good enough for you anyway."

Matt smiled at that.

"You would make such a great dad, Matt. And you'd make a terrific husband for any lady who was lucky enough to have you."

A sharp ache stabbed through my heart as visions of having to attend Matt's wedding haunted my imagination. And I'd thought Brady and Lyric's wedding was tough on me. Still, I plowed ahead, determined to do what was best for Matt. He couldn't have the woman he wanted, and he didn't want me, so there was no reason not to keep searching for Ms. Right.

I watched Matt's face as he considered my words. He was thinking about taking Jerry up on his offer.

"So, Jer," I said. "Tell me about this girl."

Jerry grinned. "Oh, she's great. Her name is Sarah Asiago."

Matt grimaced. "Like the cheese?"

"Yes. Like the cheese."

"Oh, I *love* Asiago cheese," I said with enthusiasm, as if that made her more enticing. "Almost as much as I love Parmesan cheese."

Matt chuckled as I reached for the little shaker of cheese for my pasta.

"Sarah's a big baseball fan."

"That's a red flag right there," Matt said.

"Why do you say that?" I asked.

"Where do I begin?" he said wearily. "There are all kinds of cleat chasers out there who'd just love to bag a baseball player. Believe me, that can be a lot of fun in bed."

My heart clutched in my chest. I hated hearing about the other women in Matt's bed, and I did my best to hide it.

"They get really into it, you know?" Matt continued. Unfortunately.

Jerry and Parker leaned in to listen, fascinated.

"Anything baseball-related turns them on. The uniform, balls, gloves, baseball talk, it's like they can't get enough of it."

"Wow," Parker said. "I guess I can see that. I love baseball, too. And it doesn't hurt that you have so many good-looking guys on the team."

Jerry cleared his throat and shot him a look.

"Am I wrong though?" Parker asked, holding out his hands and trying to look innocent.

"No," Jerry conceded.

"Who do you think is the hottest guy on the team?" Matt asked, sounding genuinely curious.

"Present company excluded," Parker said kindly, though

everyone knew he thought of Matt as a brother. "I'd have to say a toss-up between Brady Keaton and Trace Ridgerton."

I made a face. I adored Brady, but Trace could be kind of cocky sometimes. He reminded me of Kyle, and not in a good way.

"Good choices," Matt said with a nod.

"Sarah's not a cleat chaser," Jerry assured him. "And if you think about it, it's rather sexist to automatically think all female baseball fans are just groupies and not real sports fans."

"Hey, yeah," I said, feeling offended.

"Fair point," Matt said. "You're right. But it's also tough when a woman is a fan and knows all about you even before the first date. I mean, I guess it would be nice to date a woman who is into sports, considering what I do for a living, but sometimes it's easier if they don't follow sports at all. Then there's no question that they just want to attach themselves to your fame."

"Yeah, I can see that," I said. "Remember Brady talking about when he first met Lyric?"

Matt chuckled and nodded. "She accidentally spilled coffee all over him. Everyone else in the coffee shop was all gaga over him and she had no clue who he was."

"Sarah's not just a baseball fan, though. She's a sports fan in general. In fact, she's Director of Media Operations for the Hershey Growlers minor league hockey team."

"Huh," Matt said. "That's interesting."

"Yup," Jerry said. "She's smart and ambitious and very pretty."

Parker nodded. "That's all true. I'm not crazy about Jerry meddling in your personal life, but I will say I can vouch for her. Sarah's great. She really is. I only met her once at a Growlers game when she got us terrific seats, but she's cool."

"How do you guys know her?"

"I can't say," Jerry said, and Matt and I nodded. We knew that meant that she was his dental patient. By law, he was not allowed to disclose medical information like that.

"Look, Matt," I said. "I don't know what happened between you and that mystery college woman, and I don't want to tell you how to feel. But it's time for some tough love here. You'll regret it if you spend the rest of your life pining for someone you can't have. Hard as it is, you've got to move on if you ever hope to have the family you always wanted."

Matt nodded slowly. "You're right," he said.

Forget pasta. I needed a drink.

22

MATT

I stared at myself in the mirror, suddenly very tired. I was doing my best to muster up some enthusiasm for this date, but it wasn't easy. I finished buttoning my shirt—a dark blue one Julia said I should wear because it made my eyes "pop"—and kept staring at my reflection.

Today was a rare day off for the Baltimore Bay Birds. I was physically well-rested, but emotionally exhausted. I was tired of feeling heartsick over Julia, which was all the more reason to give tonight's date an honest shot. Jerry ... and Julia ... were right. What was I going to do, spend the rest of my life moping over a woman who only saw me as a good friend? Not only was that stupid, but it was bad for my mental health. I wasn't a perfect person by any means, but I deserved better than that.

It wasn't Julia's fault, nor was it mine that she just wasn't into me. She was totally on board with me going on this date. Julia seemed enthusiastic, hopeful that it might work out for me. Clearly, she still just saw me as a friend and probably always would.

It was time for me to move on.

I grabbed my keys and headed out the door, doing my best to psych myself up to meet Sarah. Jerry was looking out for me, and the least I could do was give his friend a chance. Still, even after all these years it was hard to picture myself with anyone but Julia. It rocked my confidence to be so utterly wrong about something like that. Being with her always felt so right. For me, anyway.

Sarah and I had decided to meet for drinks. So far, we'd only exchanged a few texts. Though I certainly didn't tell her so, I figured having a drink or two was preferable to having to sit through a whole dinner if we didn't hit it off.

I drove to the place we'd agreed on. About a half hour out of town, it was a halfway point between where she lived in Pennsylvania and my apartment in Baltimore. She was sitting at the end of the bar when I got there. I recognized her right away from the one picture I had seen—her professional photo from the Hershey Growlers website. She looked good, but I'd figured she was pretty glammed up for that photo, and I was prepared for her to be more plain in person.

Sarah turned out to be quite attractive in real life. With shoulder-length honey-blond hair and blue-green eyes, she looked like a television news anchor. She glanced up when she heard me approach.

"Matt," she said with a smile. There was no question in her voice, so she wasn't asking if I was Matt Jovey. Clearly, she recognized me. Sarah didn't seem starstruck, which was a good sign.

"So nice to meet you, Sarah," I said, offering my hand.

She shook it while keeping eye contact. Her smile was warm and friendly, and I felt at ease with her already.

"Shall we find a table to sit?" she asked, and I nodded.

"Put hers on my tab," I said. "Name's Matt."

I fished out my wallet while Sarah picked up her half-full wineglass to take to the table.

"Thanks so much," she said with another sweet smile.

Julia rarely drank wine. She was more the type to have a beer with the guys.

I chastised myself for thinking about Julia when I was on a date with another woman. The point of this date was to forget about her. To move on.

I ordered a beer for myself then scanned the room. The place wasn't too crowded, and it wasn't hard to find a table for two. There were televisions all over the place showing various sporting events, including baseball. Though I couldn't help wondering about the scores of the other teams in our division, I tried not to be rude by looking at the screens.

We sat down across from each other. It was at that point that I realized how long it had been since I'd had an actual date as opposed to a quick sexual romp in my hotel room on the road. I had no idea what to say to break the ice.

"You have such pretty eyes," Sarah said, saving me from myself. Her compliment sounded sincere and kind.

"Thanks. My friend told me to wear a blue shirt because it would bring out my eyes."

My friend. After all this time, I still wasn't used to referring to Julia that way. She was the love of my life. Stifling an annoyed sigh at myself, I forced myself to focus on the perfectly nice woman I was with.

"Well, it worked. You look great."

"I suppose it will sound insincere if I return the compliment," I said. "But you look great too, Sarah. The first thing I thought when I saw you was you look like one of those pretty TV news broadcasters."

Sarah laughed warmly. "I do have news anchor hair, for

sure. See? Barely moves."

She shook her hair and it moved only slightly.

"Industrial-strength hairspray. You need it in this humidity."

I nodded. "I'm embarrassed to tell you how much product I put in my hair."

She laughed again, which I found charming. Despite my own intensity, I'd always liked people who laughed easily.

"Oh hey, good news," Sarah said, glancing past me and up at one of the televisions. "The New York Kings are down by seven runs and it's only the third inning."

"Yeah?" I said, turning around to take a quick look at the score. I turned back around and said, "Looks like they're in for a rough night. Good."

I lifted my mug to toast New York's demise, and Sarah smiled and lifted her wineglass. We clinked and drank. I had to admit, it was fun to be with someone who was really into sports. Jerry knew what I liked. Weird how he never realized how perfect his sister was for me.

Then again, neither did she.

"You okay?" Sarah asked, looking concerned. I was angry at myself that I'd dropped my poker face there for a second.

"Oh, yeah. Sorry. That's a thing about me; I have quite the resting bitch face. Don't take it personally," I said with a laugh. She smiled again, and it warmed my heart. She was such a pleasant person. I could have a good time if I only let myself.

I took a sip of beer and glanced around the bar. "I'm sitting here trying to think of something more clever to say than just asking the normal first-date questions, but I'm coming up blank. Besides, I really do want to know the answers. Like, are you from Pennsylvania originally? Do you have brothers and sisters? Do you like your job?"

"I know what you mean about first-date questions," she said, fingering her glass. "But I'm happy to answer them. I'm from Minnesota originally."

"Really? What brought you all the way out here?"

"The job offer from the Growlers," she said. "Which leads into your other question. I majored in Business Administration with a mi nor in Sports Management because I always wanted a job in professional sports. Growing up, I developed a real love for hockey, baseball, football, you name it. Sad to say, I never had much athletic ability myself."

"So you found a way to be surrounded by the sports action without actually playing," I said, fixing my bitch face as my emotions battled for control. "That's very cool."

"Yeah, that's exactly right," Sarah said. "I love being around all that excitement, the energy of the crowd."

Julia always said the same thing, and I literally had to bite my tongue to keep from telling Sarah about "my friend."

Do not talk about another woman on a date, you idiot.

"So you like working for the Hershey Growlers? I went to a game once, but it's been a while. I see people wearing the team T-shirts all the time. Seems like they have a loyal following."

"Oh they do," Sarah said, her pretty blue-green eyes lighting up as she spoke. I'd always been attracted to passionate women. It didn't even matter what they were passionate about. I just found it sexy when they had lots going on in their own lives.

Don't even think it, I warned myself. But of course, I wasn't able to stave off thoughts about the most passionate, sexy woman I knew.

Sarah went on to talk about the Hershey Growlers and

their loyal fans, who were grateful to get some hockey action in their area even if it was minor league. She sounded excited and happy as she spoke, yet I was barely listening to her. I managed to catch the word "baseball" when she said something about wanting to work for a major league baseball team someday.

I felt terrible, not to mention pathetic, for not being able to get Julia off my mind. Here I was on a date with a perfectly lovely woman who I couldn't believe was unattached. Sarah was beautiful, smart, and kind. I barely knew her, but I had a good feeling about her. She exuded positive vibes, even if she didn't chat up the bartender and every stranger she encountered like Julia did.

I was so pissed off at myself that I nearly growled. Seriously. I almost literally roared at my own sad, pitiable behavior.

"Okay, that is more than just resting bitch face," Sarah said, looking genuinely alarmed. "Are you okay?"

"God, Sarah, I am the worst date on the planet," I grumbled.

"No you're not," she said sweetly, which only made me feel worse.

"Look, you're a really nice person—"

"Really?" Sarah asked sharply. I could see the hurt in her eyes, and my opinion of myself sank even lower. "You're giving me the brushoff already?"

She grabbed her purse and looked like she was about to storm out.

"Wait. Please. Would you let me explain?" I asked, imploring her with my eyes. I could not bear to let Sarah leave feeling rejected when this had nothing to do with her.

Sarah sighed and looked at me wearily, waiting for an explanation. I wasn't sure where to begin. In this case, it truly was a matter of *it's not you, it's me*. But how could I explain that?

"Can I level with you here? I mean, do you mind if I am totally, completely honest, which is something you should never do on a first date?"

Sarah eyed me curiously, looking less pained and more intrigued.

"Sure," she said. "Why not?"

"You are pretty and sweet and fun and smart. You've got a great job that you are clearly passionate about, and I find that sexy as hell."

Her expression softened, and she smiled tentatively. I got the feeling she wasn't sure if she believed me, but she wanted to.

"Up until I ruined it, this date was going pretty well. Feels like we're clicking, you know?"

"That's what I thought," Sarah said, sounding confused. Who could blame her?

"The truth is, I am crazily, stupidly in love with someone else and my head is totally screwed up right now."

"Oh, I see," Sarah said. The hurt in her expression switched to compassion instantly. What a sweetheart she was.

"One of those deals where we've been friends forever, you know? But I want more than that. But I don't think she does. Or maybe she might. I don't know."

I sighed heavily.

"Sarah, I am so sorry for dragging you all the way out here and wasting your time. I'll get out of your hair now. Please, stay as long as you like and order anything and put it on my tab."

I stood up to leave, but she stopped me.

"Matt," she said softly. "Please stay."

Slowly, I sank down in my chair.

Sarah reached over and took my hand. "It sounds like you could really use a friend right now. Someone to talk to. I know you don't know me very well, but it's okay to open up to me if you want."

I didn't know what it was about this woman, but I knew I could trust her. She had a way about her. Somehow, I knew she wouldn't repeat what I said to Jerry or anyone else.

"Stay. We'll have a few drinks and talk this out. If nothing else happens from this so-called date," Sarah said with a laugh, "at least maybe we'll each leave here tonight with a new friend."

"You are amazing, Sarah. I don't even know what to say."

"Let me refresh my drink, and we'll talk it all out."

"I'll get it," I said, grabbing her empty wineglass.

By the time I returned to my seat with a beer and a glass of wine, I was already second-guessing my decision to talk to a relative stranger about things I rarely spoke to anyone about.

"Tell me about her," Sarah said gently, and that now-familiar sensation of trust washed over me. I was once again struck with the certainty that she was a good woman, and I found myself wanting—needing, really—to pour out my feelings to her.

"I met her in college," I began, and then proceeded to spill my guts about *everything*. I even told Sarah about losing my virginity to Julia. Until now, I'd always lied about my first time. My story had always been that I was eighteen and still in high school when I first had sex. I went on to tell Sarah about having a chance to profess my feelings to Julia and that I'd totally blown it. With bitterness in my voice, I explained how Julia had met Kyle that same day and had been with him for years afterward.

"And now she works at Old Bay Stadium, so I see her all the time with no escape. She's the head groundskeeper there, and—"

Sarah's eyes flew open wide.

"What?" I asked, confused by her expression.

"You're talking about Jerry's sister!"

Oh shit.

I froze. I'd gotten so wrapped up in venting all my pent-up feelings that I'd totally forgotten how I'd met Sarah in the first place.

"Hey," Sarah said, reaching over to squeeze my hand. "Don't you worry. I won't breathe a word about this to anybody."

I nodded, still secure in my first impression of her. Somehow, I knew she was telling the truth. Even if she wasn't, it was too late now.

"From everything you've told me, Julia sounds like a wonderful person," Sarah said with a smile. I could hardly believe how gracious she was, and it was a relief to finally speak freely. For years, Julia had been the unnamed woman from college who broke my heart. Brady was the only other person who knew her identity, and it always felt like a weight off my chest when I got the rare opportunity to talk about how much I loved her.

"She is a wonderful person," I said.

"Do you want my advice?"

"I do, Sarah. I really do."

"Sounds to me like you have a lot of regret about not speaking up about your feelings for her in college. Matt, I think you know what you have to do now."

I sucked in a deep breath, knowing where she was going with this. And knowing she was right.

"Tell Julia how you feel. Once and for all, just tell her

everything. It's the only way you will ever be able to move on." She paused a moment, her pretty blue-green eyes filled with sympathy. I must have looked particularly pathetic. "I know it's scary, but sometimes life is scary. I think it's true that you're more likely to regret the things you didn't do rather than the mistakes you made."

I nodded.

Sarah laughed. "To be really corny and use a sports metaphor, you miss one hundred percent of the shots you don't take."

I laughed too.

"Matt," she said softly. "Take this shot. It's possible that Julia does want to be more than friends, and she may be too afraid to speak up."

It was hard to imagine Julia being too afraid of anything, but I supposed it was possible.

"Whatever happens, at least you will finally have an answer. No more wondering what if. The worst-case scenario is that she only wants to be friends."

"Do you think we could still be friends after I tell her I'm in love with her? Even if she doesn't feel the same way?"

"Yes. I do. If she's anywhere near as great as you say she is, I have no doubt she'll always be one of your dearest friends. Just talk to her, Matt. As soon as you can. Don't give her a chance to meet anyone else, and don't allow yourself to suffer any longer. Talk to her and get a straight answer, once and for all."

I swallowed the rest of my beer and set down the mug on the table. I stared at the empty glass for a moment and then nodded. I knew Sarah was right. A sense of relief washed over me just knowing that after I talked to Julia, I wouldn't have to wonder anymore.

"I hate to miss out on a charming, attractive, and not to

mention wealthy man," Sarah said with a laugh, "but I hope it works out for you."

"Thanks. So much. For everything. I know you hadn't planned on playing therapist tonight," I said apologetically.

"It's okay. We all need somebody to talk to once in a while. Let me know what happens, okay? I really want to know."

"I will."

Sarah got up to leave, then hesitated for a moment. "And if it doesn't work out ... maybe you'll give me a call?"

I stood up. "I will, Sarah. I really will. I don't mean to treat you like you're my second choice. You really are a catch. And if it wasn't for Julia, I'd definitely be asking you out on a second date."

"Thanks," she said, and I could see she appreciated my words. I'd meant what I said, too.

"You're a good guy, Matt. I'm pulling for you. I hope you get the answer you want from her."

I wanted to hug her, which was rare for me. Still, I was wary about touching women without their permission. Lucky for me, she smiled and opened her arms. I gave her a warm hug and she rubbed my back.

"Good luck," she whispered in my ear before she let go and walked out of the bar.

As I watched her leave, I couldn't help feeling tonight's date had been a success after all. If absolutely nothing else, I did get a new friend out of the deal.

At best, I'd finally gotten the balls to say to Julia what I should have said years ago.

23

JULIA

Matt's date was this weekend, and I needed a distraction or I would drive myself completely insane thinking about it. Since it was an off-day for the Baltimore Bay Birds, I decided to take a trip up to Pennsylvania to visit some of my friends I hadn't seen in a while. Jerry said I could crash at his place, which meant I could hang out with my girlfriends for as long as I wanted without having to worry about driving back to Baltimore until the morning.

I listened to loud music during the whole drive, trying to drown out thoughts of Matt going out with another woman. I knew he would tell me all about his date when I got back. What if he wound up sleeping with her? I felt like crying every time I thought about it. I was starting to think I'd made a terrible mistake telling him he should go out on that date.

What if he wound up marrying this Sarah woman? My heart squeezed in my chest when I thought about all the weddings Jerry had been responsible for so far. Knowing him, Sarah could be the perfect match for Matt. I really had been trying to do what was best for Matt, and God knows I wanted him to be happy. I was starting to wish that I'd just told Matt how I felt about him. If he'd said he only wanted to be friends, at least I would have given myself a chance to be with him.

Who was it who once said "You miss one hundred percent of the shots you don't take"? Was it Michael Jordan? Magic Johnson? Maybe it was Wayne Gretzky.

It didn't matter. I'd missed this shot big time.

If Matt wound up hitting it off with Sarah, I might regret that missed shot for the rest of my life.

Hence my need to drown my sorrows with a girl's night.

The moment I met up with Annie and Robin, my friends from college, it felt like old times. Robin and I were on the same softball team at the University of Central Pennsylvania, and Annie and I had some classes together. Annie had gotten married a few years ago, and she and her husband had bought a beautiful house out in the country.

Annie, Robin, and I packed a cooler full of drinks and hauled it down a path to an ornate gazebo located a few yards from Annie's house. It was the perfect place to unwind and catch up. The weather was lovely, hot but with a breeze that kept the air comfortable. The tension in my body began to melt away as soon as I settled in with my girls, a beer in hand.

Since my breakup with Kyle, Annie and Robin had been great about checking in with me. They expressed their concern, but had never treated me with pity, which I appreciated.

"Gimme a cocktail girl, and keep 'em coming," Annie said, her pretty, dark hair blowing in the breeze. She took the hair tie off her wrist and secured her ponytail before accepting a canned Mai Tai from Robin.

"Uh-oh," I said. "Is work that bad lately?"

"No, work is actually great," Annie said. She worked as a Lexus saleswoman, and she made *bank*. It was no wonder she could afford this gorgeous house and the surrounding acreage. "It's just that Jeff and I are gonna start trying for a kid and this is like my last hurrah. I'm on my period now, but as soon as that's done, I want my man to put a baby in me."

"Oh, that's great," I said, hoisting my bottle of beer and toasting her can. I did my best to ignore the searing pain that tore through my chest. I wanted Annie to be happy and to have the family she wanted. Of course I did. But I couldn't help thinking of Kyle and the future children I'd lost when that particular dream had ended. More painful, though, was the realization of how much I wanted Matt's baby someday.

What if he and Sarah got married and had a bunch of kids?

Why oh why did I not just tell Matt how I felt about him?

I had loved Matt for most of my life, but it took him going out with somebody else to finally admit to myself that I was *in love* with him.

"You okay?" Annie asked. She looked apologetic, probably realizing that talking about having kids might hurt me. Which it did. But it wasn't her fault I'd picked right now to realize I was head over heels in love with one of my best friends, and that I might have blown my chance with him forever.

"Oh yeah, I'm fine," I lied. I took a leisurely sip from my beer despite wanting to down the whole thing in one gulp. "Part of me hopes you get knocked up right away, but another part hopes you have to try for a while because that can be fun, too."

Annie and Robin whooped at that, and we all toasted again.

"Here's to fabulous, procreative sex," I said as we clinked our drinks. I felt better about myself because I really meant those good wishes. I was sad for me, but happy for her.

"How's your job these days, girl?" I asked Robin. She had some kind of complicated information technology job that I had never really understood. Matt, with his computer science degree, could probably explain it to me.

I groaned inwardly, realizing there was not enough alcohol in the world to make me forget him.

"It's good, it's really good," Robin said and then proceeded to tell me about whatever project she was currently immersed in. Laughing at my expression, she joked, "Did you get all that?"

"Not a damn word," I told her. "But I'm proud of you all the same."

Robin was a swinging single, and she liked it that way. I found that inspiring. Maybe I could get used to being single.

"So you're obviously kicking ass at your place of business," Annie said to me. "I can honestly say that you have the coolest, most impressive job of anybody I know."

"It really is a great job," I said, feeling a renewed sense of happiness just thinking about the beautiful Old Bay Stadium and what a dream it was to work there. I told my friends all about my crew and how exciting it was to be the boss after serving as an underling for so many years. I also spoke about my jumbotron interview, and they were suitably impressed. When I said the TV sportscasters showed me on the games sometimes, they squealed and clinked glasses with me.

It felt so great to be with my girls, and it was yet another reminder of just how much of a drag Kyle really had been on my life. Whether I wound up with Matt or anyone else for that matter, I was better off without my ex-fiancé. And that made me happy, relieved, and positively empowered.

"So Annie and I were talking," Robin said. "And we have come to the conclusion that we are the worst friends on the planet."

"Why would you say that?" I asked, grabbing another beer and popping it open.

"Because we cannot believe we have yet to go to a single Bay Birds game," Robin said.

"Oh, I understand. Life gets busy," I said with a shrug, but I had to admit it had kind of bothered me that they hadn't come to the park yet.

"We must remedy this. Now," Annie said, pulling out her phone. "Okay, finding the Bay Birds schedule ..."

"Believe me, you won't have any trouble getting tickets," I said.

"I know," Annie lamented. "I do catch some games here and there, and I know the team's not fabulous. But they'll get there. Will be all the more exciting when they finally become contenders, right?"

"I like your positive spirit," I said, toasting my friend and spilling a bit of my beer. I wasn't exactly graceful when I was buzzed. Good thing I wasn't driving anywhere. Later, I'd call a ride-share to get me to Jerry's place where I could sleep this off.

Annie and Robin both checked their schedules and they found a date when they were both free and could come to Old Bay Stadium. They bought the tickets right away, and my heart soared.

"Too bad you won't be drinking much after tonight," I said to Annie. "Otherwise, we could go party after the game like we used to after softball."

"We did have some good times," Annie said. She hadn't been on the softball team with me and Robin, but she'd partied with us anyway after our games.

"The best was after we won the championship," Robin said.

"Right?" I said excitedly as good memories came flooding back. "That was epic, but I never did touch lemon vodka after that. Ooh, that was a rough night. But it was worth it. I slept with Jackson Metcalf the next day, you know. He helped me recover from my hangover and then we got down to business."

"No you did not!" Annie exclaimed. "I thought he was with Aleigh Patterson."

"Nah uh. He met her like a month later," I said.

"You lucky bitch." Annie took a healthy swig of her cocktail. "Wish I'd gotten to hit that."

"He was good, but not as great as you might think."

"Really?" Robin asked.

"Yeah, I mean he had the body of course, but that's not everything."

Of course that just made me think of Matt, who had the body *and* the moves in bed. Gazing out onto the lush lawn, I breathed in the fresh country air. I reminded myself to be grateful for that wonderful night Matt and I had shared together, even if it never happened again.

The three of us drank more—a lot more—and got to laughing our asses off like we were still in college. I couldn't remember the last time I'd had so much fun. At one point, my eyes filled with tears not just of laughter, but of gratitude. I was sure it was partly due to the alcohol, but it was also me coming to my senses.

Hanging out with my dear friends, reminiscing about the past, and talking excitedly about the future made me truly understand how lucky I really was. I had parents and a brother who loved me dearly. I had great friends and a dream job. For the first time since Kyle dumped me, I was struck with a vital realization.

I was gonna be okay. More than okay.

My life was freakin' awesome, and I knew I had many more adventures to come. Maybe Matt would love me romantically someday and we'd get married and have kids. Or maybe that wasn't in the cards for me.

All I knew was my life was gonna kick ass whether I had a man in it or not.

Because I was gonna make sure of it.

"Cheers, bitches," I said, hoisting my beer.

"What are we cheering?" Annie said.

"To everything. To life!"

"I'll drink to that," Robin said.

And we did.

24

———

MATT

The first chance I got to talk to Julia after my date with Sarah was between innings in a game against Detroit. She was just coming off the field after she and the crew hosed down the dirt to settle the infield dust for the second half of the game. There were tons of people around, so it wasn't like we could talk privately.

"Hey, you," she said. "How was your date?"

Julia smiled, looking genuinely excited for me. That weakened my resolve considerably. Clearly, she was hoping the date had gone well.

"It was okay."

"Just okay?" she asked, cocking her head to the side.

"Yeah. I'll tell you about it later."

I did want to tell her all about it. Preferably after I'd poured my heart out to her and she'd agreed to be promoted from friend to girlfriend. I could tell her about the sweet woman named Sarah who was partly responsible for finally getting us together. That my poor date had helped me land the woman of my dreams.

"How was your girls' night?" I asked, leaning on the

metal railing of the dugout to get closer to her.

"Oh my gosh, Matt. It was great. So great," Julia said, her eyes lit up with joy. It made me feel good all over to see her happy, especially after the rough time she'd had.

"Yeah?"

"Oh yeah. We had such a blast. Drinking a lot, of course. It was like ..." She paused for a moment, as if trying to find the right words. "This will probably sound corny."

"I doubt it," I said. Julia never sounded corny. She was too genuine, too real for that.

"It was like being with them reminded me both of the good old days we had together, but also reminded me that there are plenty more good times ahead, you know? For the first time since everything went down with Kyle, I feel like I'm gonna be okay. Like, actually *okay*. Does that make sense?"

"Of course it does. I'm really glad to hear you say that."

"Yeah," she said with a smile. "I'm glad to hear me say that too. It's like, I'm gonna be just fine as a single girl. Maybe I'm even better off."

My heart sank.

But I kept my poker face.

"I feel stronger, better than I ever did with Kyle. He held me back in so many ways that I just couldn't see at the time."

I nodded but I couldn't say anything more because we were resuming play. I had to jog out to second base and do my best not to screw up the rest of the game.

Not wanting to let Brady or any of my other teammates down, I worked hard to stay laser focused while I was in the infield. The ball never got close to me anyway, and the half-inning ended with a strikeout after two high fly balls that were easily caught by the outfielders.

Once I was back in the dugout and waiting my turn to

bat, I wasn't quite so focused. As per my usual, I was second- and third-guessing my decision to tell Julia how I felt about her. Not only might she not want me as a boyfriend, she might not want *anyone*. To hear her talk, she wasn't in the market for a lover. I couldn't blame her. Julia was finally on her own after being with the same guy since she was in college. Maybe she needed space. Maybe it wasn't the right time to make a move on her.

And maybe I was chickening out, just like I had all those years ago.

I remembered Sarah's advice that since I still had so many regrets about not speaking up back then, I shouldn't make the same mistake now. That same old wave of mental and emotional exhaustion washed over me, and I knew I couldn't go on with this any longer. Sarah was right—I would never be able to move on with the rest of my life until I got a simple, straight answer about my future with Julia.

Gazing out at the field, I knew that for years, maybe for the rest of my baseball career, I would randomly catch a glimpse of Julia. My heart would clutch in my chest, and that familiar pain would spread through my body. The heartsickness and the fear of not being with her could consume me.

I had to put an end to the misery. There was no way I could go on like this.

As a heavy sense of dread filled my body, I did my best to mentally prepare for the rejection that was most likely coming my way.

It was time to put an end to the worry, the uncertainty, the madness that had plagued me since my college days.

There were way too many people around tonight, but tomorrow I would take Julia aside and tell her that I was in love with her.

25

———————

JULIA

I arrived at the ballpark super early in the morning as I so often did. I loved this peaceful time of day. Not only was it practical—I could get everything organized and ready before my crew arrived—but I loved the quiet. This time to myself gave me yet another chance to reflect on how lucky I was to be here and to get geared up and excited for the day ahead. Old Bay Stadium was the most beautiful place I'd ever seen. I loved it during the silent times and when it was roaring with excited baseball fans.

During these moments of sweet tranquility, I felt like I'd stumbled onto the key to a happy life.

Gratitude.

I was learning to be grateful for every breath, every day, and even every hardship because I learned so much from the bad times in my life. It was almost like I'd needed Kyle's rejection to teach me not to reject myself. Now I knew I didn't have to put up with anybody's half-assed support. I loved and supported my family and friends with my whole heart, and I would accept no less from people going forward. From now on, if a so-called friend or boyfriend couldn't celebrate my accomplishments as much as I celebrated theirs, I'd wish them well for their futures, but they would lose their place in my inner circle.

The sun slowly began to rise over the field, and I paused to gaze at it. Breathing in the magical scent of dirt and grass, I reveled in the beauty of it all.

I am grateful. For everything.

The sound of footsteps startled me, and I whirled around to see who was there.

"Sorry," Matt said, his lovely blue eyes apologetic for frightening me. "Wasn't trying to sneak up on you."

Putting my hand on my heart as I recovered from my scare, I said, "It's okay."

"I didn't mean to disturb your solitude."

I gazed at him, hardly bothering to conceal my longing for him. Of course he understood how magical these mornings at the stadium were for me. Because he understood me better than anyone else ever had. Or ever would. I did my best to remain grateful for having Matt as my friend, but it was hard. Every time I saw him, my pain only grew stronger. I wasn't sure how I would be able to work with him all the time, especially if he got a girlfriend. Sure, it sounded like his date with Sarah had been lackluster, but what about the next time?

"You're not disturbing me," I said. "Honestly, if it had been anybody else I might be a little annoyed. But not you. I like having you here."

"Good." He looked at me for a moment.

"You okay?"

"Yeah," he said.

But Matt wasn't okay. I knew him better than that. Something was upsetting him.

"Can I, uh, talk to you?" he asked with uncharacteristic

uncertainty. Whatever was wrong with him, I desperately wanted to fix it.

"Sure. Come with me," I said. I climbed on top of the dugout and held out my hand to help him up. Since he was a hell of a lot bigger than me it wasn't like I was much assistance. Still, I kept him steady so he wouldn't fall.

Though I had no idea what was on Matt's mind, it was obviously an uncomfortable subject. I chose to sit next to him on the dugout so he could look at me if he wanted as he spoke.

Matt let out a deep sigh.

"You know whatever it is, you can tell me," I said.

Nodding, he said, "I do know that. It's just ... hard."

I fought the temptation to tenderly rub his back in support. Instead, I kept still, waiting for him to speak. He refused to meet my gaze.

"I'm just ... tired," he said at last. "So deeply tired."

"Tired of what?"

Was he tired of playing baseball? Was he quitting the team? Dear God, was he terminally ill or something?

Panic gripped me as I waited for him to elaborate. I steeled myself, trying to emotionally prepare in case his next words were *I've been diagnosed with cancer.*

"I'm tired of pretending I'm not completely, helplessly in love with you, Julia."

Relief swept through me as I processed what he *hadn't* said before I could understand what he *did* say.

"Wait ... what?" I managed to sputter. Of all the things I'd expected, that was the very last thing on the list. I stared at him, my eyes wide. Well, I stared at his profile since he was gazing out at the field and not at me.

"I'm in love with you, Julia. And I'll understand if you only want to be close friends like we've always been. I hope to God that telling you this won't ruin our friendship, but it's just been too hard on me to have you around all the time and having to hide how I feel. I love you, and I just don't have the strength to pretend I don't anymore."

"My God, Matt," I said, and he winced. I was stunned.

Looking down and shaking his head, he said, "I'm sure this comes as a surprise. I hope this won't make things awkward for us now."

"Yeah well, you ready for another surprise?" I asked. At last, he looked at me, and his heartsick expression nearly broke me.

I tenderly caressed his face with my hand. "I'm in love with you too, Matt."

His eyes flew open wide, and he blinked.

"Surprise," I whispered.

"Y—you ..." Matt stammered, and it was positively delicious to see Mr. Cool himself caught so delightfully off guard.

"Love you. Yes, I do. So much. Now kiss me before I explode."

"Julia," he whispered. Of all the reactions he'd expected, or feared, I didn't think he'd expected me to say it back.

Taking a tantalizing few seconds to gaze intensely into my eyes, at last he pressed his lips to mine. My senses flooded with sensual, emotional memories of the passionate night we'd shared after Brady and Lyric's wedding. Matt had kissed me the same way, with raw passion and deep need. Had he been in love with me then?

Everything about Matt was both familiar and exhilarating. The scent of his cologne, his huge hands on my face, his lips devouring mine. For the first time in my life, I understood what people meant when they said a couple was truly meant to be.

Except we weren't meant to be.

A sudden, horrible thought struck my heart with such force it took my breath away. I broke off the kiss and pulled away from him.

"I can't do this," I whispered.

"What?" Matt asked. I heard the panic in his voice, and it tore my heart in two.

"I love you, Matt. I can't even begin to tell you how much. It's … It's … more than I thought possible. But I can't let myself be with you."

Shakily, I got to my feet. I was so emotionally wrecked that I was afraid I might fall off the dugout. I drew in a few breaths to steady myself.

Matt scrambled to his feet.

"Julia, what's wrong? What are you saying?"

My eyes filled with tears. "I can't be with you because sooner or later I won't be enough for you. Just like I wasn't enough for Kyle."

"Oh, sweetheart," Matt said, his face less panicked now. He looked at me with love and concern, which only made my tears come faster. "I can't imagine how badly that bastard hurt you, and I know that's not something you can get over easily. It takes time to learn to love and trust again."

"He stopped loving me," I said, my voice shaky. "And someday you will too. Oh, Matt, it'll be so much worse when it happens with you. I don't think I'd ever be able to heal from that kind of pain."

"Julia, I'm not Kyle," he said, he insisted.

"I know you're not," I told him. "Because I love you way more than I ever loved him."

Matt stared at me with those damned perfect blue eyes like he couldn't believe what I'd just said. No matter what happened, I was glad I'd told him that. He deserved to know.

"I will *never stop loving you,*" Matt said, looking and sounding more intense than ever before. And that was really saying something.

There was no way I could be with Matt, but he deserved to know why.

"You say that now, Matt. But you will. Sooner or later, you'll realize I'm not enough for you." He started to protest, but I held up my hand to stop him. "For a *really* long time, your mind and heart have been totally messed up over the woman from college that broke your heart. One day you'll wake up and remember that she's still the only one you want, and that will be the end of me. Of us. I just ... I couldn't take that, Matt. So I need to end this between us before it begins."

My heart shattering into a million pieces, I knew I had to get out of there. I made it to the edge of the dugout when I heard Matt cry out, "You're the woman from college, Julia!"

I froze, not understanding what he was telling me. I turned around slowly. "What are you talking about?"

Matt smiled, and I saw both relief and amusement in those eyes I loved so much.

"*You* are the woman from college," he repeated. "The one who broke my heart. The one I never got over. The one I never will get over."

"No. No, no, no," I said. "She was somebody you met after I left school. That's what you told me!"

Matt shook his head. "No, I didn't. You and Jerry just assumed it was somebody I met after you graduated, and that's why you never met her. I never said that. I just never corrected you when you said it."

My mind whirred as I thought back to all the times we'd

talked about this mystery woman. And all the times Matt had clammed up at the mere mention of the girl, never offering a name or any details. It wasn't possible that she was *me*. Was it?

I stared at Matt, trying to understand. He opened his arms, and I went into them.

"All this time, it's been you, Julia. You are the one I love. The one I always loved. That's why I said I was so tired of fighting my feelings for you."

"Was this ... is this because I spent that night with you in college? A lot of people get emotionally attached to their first, you know."

Matt shook his head and tenderly ran his fingers through my hair. "I was already in love with you by the time we slept together."

"You were?" I asked, still trying to wrap my head around what Matt was telling me.

"Yes. Then when we got back from South Beach, we had lunch together. I was gonna ask you to be my girlfriend, but I lost my nerve." His face darkened with pain. "You met Kyle that very afternoon. And you were with him for the next six years."

"Oh my God," I whispered. It was finally dawning on me how much Matt had suffered all these years. Through my dating Kyle and then my engagement. I couldn't even fathom how painful that must have been for him. No wonder he was tired.

"You don't have to worry, Julia," Matt said, gazing at me with such tender affection that it made my knees go weak. "After all these years, try as I might, I never figured out how to stop loving you."

And that's when I knew I would remember this moment for as long as I lived. Standing there on top of the dugout at

Old Bay Stadium, the sun rising around us, I knew I would spend the rest of my life with Matt Jovey.

"I love you so much, Matt."

"Thank God," was his relieved response, making me laugh.

Matt dipped his head to kiss me again, as if sealing the deal. After aching for his touch for so long, I could not get enough of him. And I still could not believe that I was the infamous woman from college. The woman of Matt's dreams.

Me.

This was positively unreal. And I never wanted this moment to end.

"Make love to me, Matt," I cried.

"Yes," he said through clenched teeth, the need clear in his voice and his body. "Let's go to my place."

"No. Do it to me here. Now. Right here on top of the dugout."

He looked at me like I was nuts.

"You're with *me* now, Matt Jovey. You're gonna have to get used to my insanity."

"I *love* your insanity," he said. His eyes sparkled, and I knew he meant those words. "But this is just a little too insane for comfort."

"Come on, Matt," I pleaded. "It would be amazing to have sex right here on top of the dugout. Every time we look over here during a game, we'll remember what we did. Every time we see the dugout on TV, we'll know that's right where you took me with complete abandon."

My urge to mate with the love of my life here and now was nearly uncontrollable. He would have a tough time talking me out of this one, and he knew it.

Watching his face carefully, I knew he was torn between

being uncomfortable with the idea and really wanting to do it.

He glanced around the place and sighed. Gazing skyward, he said, "Julia, there are hotel buildings right across the street that look directly into the stadium. People can see us here. They could take *pictures*."

Dammit. Matt had a good point. That was why we were so good for each other. I was rhyme and he was reason.

"Hold on," he said. "I have an idea."

He climbed down from the dugout and then helped me down. Taking my hand, Matt led me into the dugout. He stared at the dirty floor. "Hmmm. I guess I didn't really think this through."

"You're thinking we should do it in the dugout? I love that, Matt. That is so hot."

"It's public but not too public, and you can still see the dugout all the time and on TV like you said."

I smiled, deeply touched by Matt's thoughtfulness. Already, being with him was completely different from being with Kyle. He would have told me my dugout idea was nuts and that would have been the end of it. Not only did Matt tolerate my crazy, I think he liked it.

"We'd be more or less hidden from view down here," Matt said, his hands on his hips as he surveyed the dugout like a contractor trying to solve a problem. "But the floor is so dirty."

"You think I care about that?"

Matt looked up at me and smiled. And it wasn't just any old smile. It was an *I love you so much, Julia* smile.

"That's my rugged, outdoorsy girl."

"Yes," I said, coming closer to him. "I am your girl."

Matt sighed softly. "I can't believe it."

"And as your girl," I said, kissing his neck, "I command you to have your way with me, here and now."

He dipped his head and kissed me. Before long, we were going at it hot and heavy.

"Hold up a second," he said, breaking off the kiss. Matt looked down at the floor again. He was worried about how messy it was, even if I wasn't.

"Matt, I told you I don't care about—"

"No, I know. But I can't have you lay down on the concrete with nothing underneath you. Especially your head. Don't go anywhere," he said with a grin.

With that, he dashed into the clubhouse. I chuckled as I watched him go, loving his practical side as much as he seemed to like my impulsiveness.

"Okay," he said when he emerged from the locker room. "These should help."

Matt had a seat cushion in one hand and a towel in the other. He carefully placed them on the floor of the dugout for me.

"Perfect," I said, my heart and body desperate for Matt's touch.

We picked up where we left off. He kissed me passionately and forcefully, and soon my panties were drenched with my desire for him.

"I need you, Julia," he said in a tone of voice that told me he meant business. God I loved when he spoke through clenched teeth that way, like he could barely control himself around me.

Pushing me down on the ground of the dugout, he grabbed my shorts and panties and yanked them off in one quick move. Matt was so *dominant*, and it drove me wild. Now I knew that intensity was driven by genuine love for me, which made this experience even more thrilling than the last time.

He took off his shorts and underwear and then pressed his cock against my clit. I moaned as he ground against my most sensitive spot. I was so painfully aroused, I nearly came. Then he shifted his cock away. It was torture, but I knew the wait for satisfaction would be worth it.

Matt reached behind me and unclasped my bra. Rubbing my breasts, he left my shirt on and my bra hanging open, which was even more exciting than if he'd stripped me totally naked. Like he couldn't wait another moment to take me, and there was no time to take off my clothes.

Without warning, Matt rammed his cock into me. The burst of pleasure was so intense that I screamed with delight.

"*Shhh*," Matt said. He glanced around nervously, but I saw the pride in his eyes.

"You know ..." I panted, "that I can't be quiet during sex. Especially ... with ... *you* ..."

Last time we'd had sex at his place, I made sounds I'd never made before in bed.

Matt grinned, and I'd never seen him look hotter. He grabbed my leg and threw it over his shoulder, clearly remembering how much I'd liked that position the last time.

His lips said be quiet, but his actions made me scream.

I opened my mouth to cry out with sheer sexual bliss, and he quickly kissed me to shut me up. Thrusting in perfect rhythm, Matt Jovey rocked my world right there in the Baltimore Bay Birds dugout. Later tonight, it would be filled with sweaty baseball players surrounded by thousands of fans, none of whom would have any idea the second baseman had banged the head groundskeeper on the floor.

It was by far the most thrilling sexual experience of my life, but I knew if I didn't have an orgasm soon, I would die.

"Matt," I pleaded. "Oh God, I need to come. Please make me come. *Please* ..."

Slipping his fingers between my legs, he rubbed my clit. Somehow, Matt managed to keep thrusting inside me, finger my clit, and cover my cries with his mouth all at the same time.

Good thing he was able to muffle my scream when I came because all of Baltimore would have heard it. I came and came and came underneath Matt's expert fingers. I was so lost in my own bliss that I didn't even notice when Matt finished. I knew he had since I could feel the warmth of the generous amount of semen he'd pumped into me. I'd never been so grateful for the pill, since it allowed me to experience every naked inch of my darling boyfriend's body.

"Julia," Matt murmured softly, tenderly, in my ear. He slid his strong arms underneath me, holding me close and protecting me from the hard ground.

Yet another reason to be hopelessly in love with Matt. He was powerful and forceful during sex, and tender and loving afterward. And I knew it wasn't only after-sex tenderness. It was his way all the time. He was a man of few words, but I knew he would always have my back. He would celebrate my accomplishments and mourn my defeats, and I would do the same for him. From this day forward. Always.

Matt hoisted himself off me and quickly got dressed before sliding my panties and shorts back on me. I sat up and re-clasped my bra. Gazing out at the ballfield, he breathed a sigh of relief that we'd gotten away with having sex in public. I loved that Matt had done this for me, but I didn't enjoy stressing him out.

"Can we go somewhere a little more private now?" he asked.

"Yes. How 'bout we stop by my place so I can grab a few things. Then I can stay at your place tonight. If that's okay."

Matt laughed, sounding positively giddy. I was honored that I seemed to be one of the few people who could provoke an emotional reaction from him.

"Of course it's okay."

Kissing him softly, I said, "Good. Because I don't want to be away from you for a single second."

Matt gazed into my eyes. "Now you know how I've felt all these years."

I nodded, running my fingers through his hair.

My head was still reeling from the knowledge that I, Julia Frederick, was the woman that Matt had been pining for all this time. As we walked out of the stadium hand-in-hand, I thought about how hard it must have been to watch me with Kyle. I'd been so oblivious, and God knows how many things I might have said and done that had unintentionally hurt him.

Squeezing his hand tight, I resolved to spend the rest of my life making up for lost time. I would do everything in my power to make sure Matt never doubted my love for him.

26

MATT

Today was the proverbial first day of the rest of my life. I'd shouldered the heavy weight of unrequited love for so long that my body felt physically different now. I felt lighter and happier, with a sense of hope and excitement for the future.

Shaking my head as I grabbed my gear from the clubhouse locker, I kept waiting to wake up from this dream. I walked out to the dugout that we had christened with our lovemaking this morning, still feeling her touch on my skin.

Julia Frederick was in love with me.

This was no dream. This was my life now.

With a renewed sense of energy, I was more than ready to take on the New York Kings, our most despised rivals.

Julia and I searched for each other throughout the game to share a private gaze. We weren't hiding our relationship or anything, we just hadn't told anyone yet. Though I was usually a very private person, I felt like standing on top of the dugout and shouting that Julia loved me. I felt like professing my love in big letters on the jumbotron.

I chuckled to myself. Julia would love that. Where I was

private, she was public. Hence, our copulation in the Bay Birds dugout. Where I was intense, she was free-spirited. We were two halves of a whole.

Well, not exactly. Julia had said she was okay with being single, and that was a good thing. She was a complete person before she hooked up with me, and that was as it should be. I was the one who needed to work on being a whole person, considering how obsessed I'd been with her for so long. In the best relationships, two people complement each other. Not complete another person so much as highlight them. Celebrate them. That was how Julia and I always had been as friends, and that would not change now that we were lovers.

We were good for each other. And that was what mattered.

As the perfect capper to a surreal day, I hit a two-run homer against the Kings in the eighth inning, and we went on to win the game by exactly two runs.

"You had a good day, huh?" Brady said, clapping me on the back as we walked into the clubhouse after the game.

"Dude, you have *no* idea," I said with a grin.

"What are you up to, ya sly bastard?" he asked suspiciously.

I sat on the metal bench so I could take off my cleats and put my regular shoes on. I glanced around at the rest of the guys, but nobody was paying any attention to us. Not that it mattered. Soon enough, everyone would know that Julia and I were an item.

"I told Julia how I felt about her," I said.

"Yeah?" Brady said, eyes filled with hope for me.

I nodded. "Turns out she feels the same way. We're together now. In fact, we were *together* this morning."

"No shit!" Brady said. "That's great, Matt."

Julia was never shy about sex, so I knew she wouldn't mind me mentioning it. She'd probably tell more people than I did.

"It sure is," I said. "Still can't quite believe it."

"Man, I am so happy for you," he said, and I knew he meant it.

"Thanks. For everything."

Brady nodded. "You know I got your back."

"Yeah. I do know that."

I grabbed the rest of my gear and eagerly headed out. Though I could hardly wait to get home to my place where Julia would stay tonight, I took the time to sign some autographs for the fans before I left the stadium. I did it mostly because it was the right thing to do, but partly because it wasn't often that I'd been the hero of the game. I needed to enjoy it while it lasted.

With Julia cuddled up next to me, I slept better than I had in a long time. When I woke up in the morning, it took me a few seconds to remember everything that had transpired yesterday. Then it hit me all over again that Julia loved me.

I made breakfast while she showered, surprising her with my homemade eggs Benedict. Naturally, I made the hollandaise sauce with generous dashes of Old Bay.

"This is amazing," Julia said after swallowing her first mouthful. "You are a man of many talents."

Julia, too, had innumerable talents, but cooking was not one of them. Yet another instance of how we complemented each other.

"Glad you like it," I said.

After breakfast, we lingered at the door, kissing our

goodbyes. Julia had laundry and other things to do at her apartment and then she needed to go to the ballpark. Though I would have loved it if she wanted to move in with me right away, I didn't want to push things. I'd loved her forever, but her loving me was still new to her. She might need some time. Besides, as long as we were together, it didn't matter where we lived.

Once Julia left, I picked up the phone to call Sarah. She'd been a tremendous help to me, and she deserved a clear answer on where we stood. She was a nice person, and I really might have gone for her had I not just landed the woman of my dreams. Sarah was probably better off without me, anyway. She would have always known she wasn't my first choice, and she deserved a man who loved her with his whole heart. I hoped she would find a great guy someday.

"Hey, Sarah. It's Matt."

"Matt! How are you?" I heard the smile in her voice, and I felt guilty.

"I'm doing well. And you?"

"I'm fine. So, spill it. Did you talk to Julia?"

"I did," I said, wincing as I spoke. It was silly. Sarah barely knew me, and it wasn't like she would be crushed that I was taken. Still, I wasn't good at breaking bad news. "And it went really well."

"Oh, I'm so glad to hear that," Sarah said, and it sounded like she meant it. "What did you say? What did *she* say?"

"You'd have been proud of me," I said, remembering Sarah's encouragement. "I laid it all on the line. Figured I might as well go for it, so I told her that I'd been in love with her for a long time, and I was worn out from trying to hide it."

"And?"

"And she said she was in love with me, too."

"Oh, Matt," Sarah said dreamily. I wasn't proud of it, but my ego was slightly wounded that she wasn't more upset. "That's so lovely."

Her kindness meant a lot to me, and I got the feeling she was the hopeless romantic type. Initially, I'd intended on sparing her the details, but now I got the impression she wanted to know more.

"It was incredible. I didn't expect her to say it back, but she did."

"I'm so happy for you, Matt. I can't tell you how glad I am that it worked out for you," Sarah said. And there it was. I heard the note of wistfulness in her voice, and I felt terrible. I didn't know if the hint of sadness was over me or if it was because Sarah wanted what Julia and I had.

"I really appreciate all your advice, Sarah. I don't know that I would ever have had the guts to finally speak up if it hadn't been for you."

"I'm glad I could help," she said.

"So, how's work going?" I asked, not wanting to rub my good fortune in her face any longer than necessary.

"It's good," Sarah said enthusiastically. "We had a great game last night. The Growlers won in a blowout, and it was plush toy giveaway night, which meant there were lots of happy kids in the stands."

"That sounds fun. Nothing makes the job more worthwhile than seeing happy little sports fans," I said, smiling as I recalled signing a ball for a little boy last night who'd been wearing my jersey. I'd been thrilled that he saw me hit that two-run homer and then got to meet me after the game. His excitement was yet another thing that made yesterday awesome.

Sarah and I talked on the phone for forty-five minutes,

and not out of guilt on my part. Turned out we really did hit it off as friends, and I genuinely enjoyed our conversation. I was grateful Jerry had introduced us, and I told her so.

"Me too, Matt," she said. "You're a great guy. Maybe we can get together for dinner again. With Julia, of course. I'd love to meet her."

"I would love that. I told her all about our date and how I ruined it. And how cool you were about it."

Sarah laughed, and I felt the warmth of her kindness over the phone. "That's great. Gotta run for now. Talk to you later, okay?"

"Sounds good. Take care."

I felt relieved that I'd been honest with Sarah. With the hard part over, I was happy that I'd found a new friend. Sarah was a terrific woman, and double dating with her and Julia might be fun. I tried to think of someone on the team to set her up with, but nobody immediately came to mind.

Julia came over after the game to spend the night again. We made love in my bed, and this time I took my time with her.

Plus, she could make all the noise she wanted.

She cried out with pleasure during sex, and she screamed my name a lot. Sex with Julia was far better than it ever had been with any other woman. I *loved* how into it she was. With all those other women, I'd always fantasized that I was with Julia. Now the fantasy was reality, and I still couldn't believe this was my life now.

"Mmmm," Julia moaned as she lay back in bed, reveling in postcoital bliss. "You are *sooo* good, Matt."

"I do my best," I said, kissing her sweet mouth before settling in bed beside her.

"You know," Julia said lazily, "somebody's gonna have to tell Jerry about this."

"Not it!" we both yelled at the same time.

Julia giggled, and I pulled her closer.

Jerry would flip out if he knew about the things I'd been doing to his sister lately. But Julia was right. We had to tell him.

27

———

JULIA

We figured it would be safest to meet Jerry in a public place, so we chose his favorite steak joint for dinner. Ever since Matt's date with Sarah, Jerry had been bugging him about why it hadn't worked out. He'd been so sure she and Matt would hit it off, which they kind of did. Sarah sounded like a cool person, and she and Matt had become good friends since they went out for drinks that night. It was because of her that Matt had finally professed his love for me. He'd told me Sarah had helped him realize he would never be able to move on with his life until he finally took a chance with me.

I owed Sarah big time, and I looked forward to meeting her.

Matt had taken great care to explain to me that though there was nothing romantic between the two of them, he kept in contact with her. He wanted to make sure there were no misunderstandings about that, and honestly, it didn't bother me at all that they were friends. I had lots of guy friends, and Matt had no problem with that either. I was grateful that Matt had been up front about her, though.

Being friends was fine. Keeping that information from me wouldn't have been. Now, every time Matt looked down at his phone and cracked a smile, I knew Sarah had probably sent him another funny meme. He always showed them to me, and they made me laugh. Clearly Sarah and I had a similar sense of humor.

"Sarah's great," Matt said to Jerry when we sat down to dinner. My brother had started in with the inquisition right away. Lucky for us, Sarah had been discreet about everything she and Matt had discussed that night. "She's just not for me."

"I don't get it," Jerry said. "She's perfect for you."

"Jer," Parker said gently. "Let it go already. Matt was a good sport about going on the date, but it didn't work out."

"Yeah," Jerry said suspiciously. "I'm just not sure *why* it didn't work out. Could be they weren't compatible, which is unlikely. Or it could be because he's still hung up on that tramp from college."

I giggled and watched with amusement as Matt stifled a laugh.

The server brought our drinks, and Matt and I waited until Jerry had some beer in him before we broke the news. I made eye contact with Matt, and he nodded. No time like the present.

"The truth is, Jerry, the reason it didn't work out between Matt and Sarah is that he found someone else," I said.

"Really?" Jerry asked, shocked. He eyed Matt curiously.

"Yes," I said. "He met someone that he cared deeply for ..." Matt nodded and smiled as he gazed at me. "And the great thing is, I met someone, too."

"You did?" Parker asked. "That's great, Julia. I'm really happy to hear that."

Parker smiled warmly at me. He'd always treated me like

the sister he never had, and I knew he'd been worried about me after my engagement broke up.

"Yeah, it's so great that we both met someone who can make us happy," I said, drawing in a deep breath. Holding my gaze, Matt reached over and took my hand and kissed it, just like we'd rehearsed ahead of time. Then I turned to Jerry to see his reaction.

His eyes flew open wide.

I squeezed Matt's hand before letting go.

"Wh—what—what is going on here?" Jerry said, sounding almost panicked.

"It makes sense, Jerry," Parker soothed. "They've known each other for a long time."

It was funny how Parker seemed pleased yet not at all surprised that Matt and I were together.

"Yeah, as friends. We grew up together," Jerry said, clearly still in shock.

"Feelings can change over time," Matt said. "We're more than friends now."

"You're *doing* my *sister*?" Jerry said in a voice that was way too loud for a nice restaurant.

Both Matt and Parker cringed with embarrassment, while I was practically doubled over with laughter.

"Jerry, you gotta chill," I said, still giggling.

My brother glanced around the restaurant, finally remembering we were in public.

"Sorry, sorry," he mumbled.

Then he turned to glare fiercely at Matt. "I know how you are, Matt. Now that you're a big shot ballplayer, you've had women in every city your team visits."

"This isn't like that," Matt assured him. "I'm in love with Julia."

"That's wonderful," Parker said, smiling at me.

"Thanks," I told him. Thank God Parker was here. Maybe he could keep my brother calm.

"What about that bimbo from college you're still so messed up over?" Jerry said, still clearly pissed. And I loved him for it. Matt was his nearest and dearest friend, but I knew Jerry would kill him if he ever hurt me. Between Matt's history of sleeping around and his being obsessed with that other woman, I couldn't blame him for worrying about me.

Thumbing toward myself, I said, "That would be me. I'm the bimbo!"

Pretty sure I said that too loud for the quiet restaurant, too. Matt smirked, looking amused. He never tried to shut me up when I was being too loud. I loved that about him.

"What are you talking about?" Jerry asked.

"Julia was the woman from college," Matt explained gently. "She's the one who got away. The one I've been hung up on my whole life."

"No," Jerry said, shaking his head vehemently. "It was some woman you met after Julia left the school."

"I never said that. Everybody just figured it must have been some woman I met after Julia already got her degree, otherwise Julia would have known her."

Matt paused for a moment, giving Jerry time to process the truth.

"I've been in love with Julia for a really long time, Jerry. But for years she belonged to somebody else."

"That must have been incredibly hard on you, Matt," Parker said.

"It was," he said. "I can't even begin to tell you how painful it's been for me."

I put my hand on Matt's back and rubbed it tenderly.

"And you know I've always loved Matt like a friend," I

said. "But my feelings have changed for him, and now he's my lover. You're gonna have to accept that, Jerry."

Jerry winced but nodded. He was never great about discussing my love life, and I knew my being with his best friend was totally weird for him. But he'd better get used to it.

"She's really the one you've been in love with all this time?" Jerry asked uncertainly.

"Believe me," I said. "I had no idea either. But I love him, too. Very much."

Matt and I gazed into each other's eyes for a moment, and then I turned back to my brother.

"Jerry," I told him. "He's *my* Parker."

That got through to him. I could see it in his eyes. *That* he understood.

"Okay," Jerry said softly, and I knew it really was okay.

The server brought our food, and everything felt right in my world.

28

MATT

It didn't take long for word to spread that Julia and I were a couple, especially once I gave Brady the go-ahead to tell people. Everybody was crazy about Julia, and the guys on the team seemed happy to see us together. Angel pulled me aside and told me he always suspected we were more than friends. After she broke up with Kyle, anyway. What really surprised me was that his suspicions were mostly due to the way Julia looked at *me*. I guess she'd been as good at hiding her feelings as I had been, because I'd had no clue she was into me.

The Baltimore Bay Birds finished out the season toward the bottom of the standings. Though not unexpected, it still sucked. I tried to look on the bright side. I took pride in being a part of the rebuilding of the team, and next year things might be different.

After the season was over, Julia gave up her apartment and moved all her stuff into my place. Well, *our* place. She kept busy over the fall and winter doing some volunteer work, among other things. She thoroughly enjoyed not having to get a second job in the off-season for once. Her big-league salary was enough. I considered doing some volunteer work with her but decided that my presence and fame might be too much of a distraction. Besides, most of the work Julia did was with young girls and teens, teaching them how to be women leaders in any field they chose to work in. Though I supported that mission wholeheartedly, I didn't exactly have any personal experience to offer.

We made the best of the off-season, spending time with Jerry and Parker as well as with my family. Julia had a little too much fun with sexual innuendos designed to drive her brother mad, but it provided much entertainment and lively dinner conversation. As always, Julia's presence made everything more fun.

Our relationship was weird for my family, too. They'd always thought of Julia as my sister, like most people did, but it didn't take them long to come around. My mother in particular was thrilled to see me so happy with a woman.

By the time winter was over, Julia and I were both eager to get back to the ballpark. With the snow gone, she had plenty of work to do to get the field back in shape for the season. And before we knew it, I was headed off to spring training in Florida.

While I was down in Florida, I called Sarah for two reasons. One, to tell her about a job opportunity, and two, I needed her advice on something. Something important.

"I'm not sure," Sarah said after I'd explained to her about the Director of Community Partnerships and Events position with the Baltimore Bay Birds that I'd recently heard about.

"Really?" I was puttering around my hotel room, bored and missing Julia. She would be my next phone call after I hung up with Sarah. I was horny as hell, and nobody did phone sex better than my girl. Listening to her give herself an orgasm over the phone made my jerking off alone in my room a lot more satisfying. I started to get caught up in imagining Julia pleasuring herself and had to force myself to remember I was supposed to be having a conversation with somebody else.

"Yeah," Sarah said.

"I'm surprised to hear you say that," I said. "I think you'd be perfect for the job. And you always said you wanted to work for a major league ball club."

"That is true," Sarah said uncertainly. "And I've heard nothing but good things about working for the Baltimore Bay Birds."

"They are a great organization. I can vouch for that."

We talked a little more about the job, and she promised to at least consider it.

"And did you say there was something else you wanted to ask me?" Sarah said as we wrapped up our discussion about the Director of Community Partnerships and Events job.

"Yes. I need your professional events planning advice. It's about Julia ..."

29

JULIA

We were a few weeks into the baseball season, and the Baltimore Bay Birds were holding their own. They still weren't great, but they were getting there. And it felt amazing to be out on the field again. Now that it was late April, the days were getting warmer again, which I loved.

Breathing in the fresh air at the start of today's game, I was filled with the sense of gratitude that was still with me after all this time. I'd had this glorious job for more than a year, and I never took a single second of it for granted. Matt and I were more in love than ever, and it was so cool that we could share our mutual love of baseball. We agreed that we'd rather be on the field than anywhere else in the world.

After the fifth inning ended, I dispatched my crew to drag the infield. By this time in the game, the players had scuffed it up pretty good, so we needed to quickly and efficiently smooth it out for the guys. Me and the crew raced out onto the field with our large metal drags. Those things are razor sharp on the bottom, so we had to be careful. We got everything all fixed up and ready to go for the next inning.

Or so I'd thought.

Suddenly, every member of my crew froze. They just stopped in place, staring at me. It was so bizarre. I glanced behind me to see what the hell they were all looking at. I was afraid an idiot had jumped out of the stands and onto the field. But there was nothing there.

One by one, each crew member let go of their metal drags. Just left them there on the field as they stared at me. With their baseball caps pulled down to obscure their faces, I couldn't see their expressions to search for clues about what was happening.

"What is this, a mutiny?"

Terror struck my heart. There were more than 30,000 fans watching this spectacle, whatever it was.

One by one, each member of my crew dropped down to one knee. Then, one by one, they each stood back up again. All but one man. The man on his knee took off his baseball cap.

It was Matt.

I gasped, suddenly understanding what was happening. I walked over to him on shaky legs.

Gazing up at me, he held out a ring box.

"Julia Frederick, you've brought crazy to my life for as long as I've known you. I've been crazy in love with you since we were both so young. I love your special blend of insanity and fun and passion. Will you marry me and keep making me crazy for the rest of my life?"

My eyes filled with tears.

Some people hated public proposals, especially baseball scoreboard proposals. People think they're hokey.

But they're not. Not for the right people.

I adored this field, and Matt knew that. He was wildly uncomfortable with a public spectacle, but he knew I loved it. I could not begin to imagine how stressful this must have been for him, but he'd done it anyway. For me.

"Yes!" I exclaimed. "Of course I will. And thanks for proving you can be crazy too sometimes."

I offered my hand, and he slid the ring on. The crowd went *insane,* and I knew the scoreboard was displaying "She said YES!"

And then fireworks, actual *fireworks* went off for a few seconds, and I realized how much planning had gone into this.

Matt stood up and kissed me, and the crowd went wild all over again.

We'd christened this beautiful ballpark in every way. I'd fallen in love with Matt here. We'd had sex in the dugout. And here on the field, we'd declared to the world that we would spend the rest of our lives together.

Dear God, did I ever love this place. And I loved Matt.

And I fucking loved baseball.

30

———

MATT

A few days after I proposed, Julia headed up to Pennsylvania to spend the day with Annie and Robin. She took Lyric with her, and she was excited to introduce one of her newest friends to her old college buddies. I was headed out on a road trip with the team in a few hours, so right now I had the place to myself. To use the time wisely, I cooked a bunch of meals to freeze for us to eat once we got back home.

The television was on in the kitchen as I worked, and the sports channels were still going crazy over my proposal. I had given the TV crew a heads up to keep rolling, otherwise they never would have taped the groundskeeping crew fixing the infield. The prospect of my proposal being broadcast on live television had terrified me, but I'd known Julia would love it. That had made all the planning and the stress worth it. I'd never forgotten the look of disappointment on her face when she talked about Kyle's proposal. I swear, it was like that jerk didn't know her at all.

I'd taken a lot of good-natured teasing from my team, but I didn't care. The whole thing had been *way* out of my comfort zone, but I knew I'd never regret it. The baseball field was her favorite place on the planet, and she was so proud of her job. Rightfully so. The team got all the glory when we won, and it was so easy to forget all the workers who toiled tirelessly behind the scenes. Except for the time they interviewed her for the jumbotron and the occasional quick glimpse on TV, most baseball fans didn't know who she was. Now they would, since they'd seen her hard at work on the field when I'd asked her to marry me.

I could only hope that being engaged to the second baseman for the Baltimore Bay Birds wouldn't overshadow the important work she did. Even if she decided to change her last name when we married, I wanted the world to know her as Julia Frederick, head groundskeeper for the Baltimore Bay Birds. Expert caretaker of the most beautiful park in all of baseball.

My phone buzzed with a text. Glancing at it, I saw it was from Sarah telling me she'd accepted the Director of Community Partnerships and Events job for the Baltimore Bay Birds.

"Sweet," I said out loud as I wrapped up the casserole I'd made so I could store it in the freezer.

It would be awesome to have her join the Bay Birds organization. I made a mental note to text her my congratulations and to try to nail down a date when Julia and I could take her out for a congratulatory dinner.

I chuckled as I listened to the sportscasters on ESPN talk about my proposal. After putting the casserole away, I stopped to watch the broadcast for a moment. I never liked seeing myself on television, but it was a necessary evil sometimes when I was trying to dissect my swing and figure out how to improve. This time, it didn't bother me so much to watch. I guess because the outcome—gaining Julia's hand in marriage—made it all worthwhile.

I had to admit, it made for riveting entertainment. The grounds crew had been in on it of course, as were the scoreboard operators and the higher-ups, including the owner. I hadn't wanted to get Julia in any trouble with my stunt, so I'd cleared it with management. The announcers had been taken totally by surprise. At first, they'd been excited when they realized that it was Julia being proposed to. They identified her—loud and clear on local TV that had now gone national—as Julia Frederick, head groundskeeper of the Baltimore Bay Birds. I knew she got a kick out of that, as well she should.

Then, when I took off my cap, the announcers had gone positively *ballistic*.

"Holy cow, that's Matt Jovey! The Bay Birds second baseman!" one of them shouted.

My dating Julia was common knowledge around the clubhouse, but nobody in the media had known about us. They did now.

Of course, after they realized who I was, the attention had shifted to me. That sucked and it wasn't fair to Julia, but there was nothing we could really do about it. At least our engagement had drawn attention to the incredible work she did for the team, and I was proud to see her get some well-deserved recognition.

It hadn't occurred to me until just now, but my public proposal was a nice, final "fuck you" to Kyle. What a great way to show the whole world that Julia had moved on and would never look back. She had an awesome job and a guy who loved her the way she deserved.

Kyle's loss was my gain.

And everybody had thought I was crazy to hold on to my

love for that woman from college all this time. Sometimes patience paid off.

And Julia had been well worth the wait.

THANK you so much for reading the second book in The Boys of Baltimore Series. I hope you will continue on with the next book in the series, Called Third Strike.

Heartfelt thanks to you for reading!